'Jack, romance, love, lust, whatever you call it, it makes the world go round.'

There was a beat of silence from Jack. 'You really think so?'

'Certainly.' Geena knew her tone lacked conviction but they were talking about him here. 'And just as obviously you don't.'

He chuckled but then his smile died. 'I'm no teenager, Geena. I've been there and done that!'

Leah Martyn's writing career began at age eleven, when she wrote the winning essay in the schoolwork section of a country show. As an adult, success with short stories led her to try her hand at a longer work. With her daughter training to become a Registered Nurse, the highs and lows of hospital life touched a chord, and writing Medical Romances liberally spiked with humour became a reality. Home is with her husband in semi-rural Queensland. Her hobbies include an involvement with live theatre and relaxing on the beach with a good book.

Recent titles by the same author:

A COUNTRY CALLING

ALWAYS MY VALENTINE

BY
LEAH MARTYN

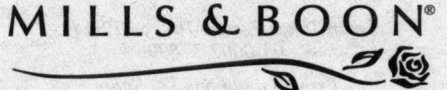

DID YOU PURCHASE THIS BOOK WITHOUT A COVER?

If you did, you should be aware it is **stolen property** as it was reported *unsold and destroyed* by a retailer. Neither the author nor the publisher has received any payment for this book.

All the characters in this book have no existence outside the imagination of the author, and have no relation whatsoever to anyone bearing the same name or names. They are not even distantly inspired by any individual known or unknown to the author, and all the incidents are pure invention.

All Rights Reserved including the right of reproduction in whole or in part in any form. This edition is published by arrangement with Harlequin Enterprises II B.V. The text of this publication or any part thereof may not be reproduced or transmitted in any form or by any means, electronic or mechanical, including photocopying, recording, storage in an information retrieval system, or otherwise, without the written permission of the publisher.

This book is sold subject to the condition that it shall not, by way of trade or otherwise, be lent, resold, hired out or otherwise circulated without the prior consent of the publisher in any form of binding or cover other than that in which it is published and without a similar condition including this condition being imposed on the subsequent purchaser.

MILLS & BOON and MILLS & BOON with the Rose Device are registered trademarks of the publisher.

First published in Great Britain 2000
Harlequin Mills & Boon Limited,
Eton House, 18-24 Paradise Road, Richmond, Surrey TW9 1SR

© Leah Martyn 2000

ISBN 0 263 81944 2

Set in Times Roman 10½ on 12½ pt.
03-0002-37899

Printed and bound in Spain
by Litografia Rosés S.A., Barcelona

CHAPTER ONE

'OK, WHO'S the joker?' Charge Nurse Geena Wilde tilted her dark head enquiringly towards her team on the early shift at Hopeton District Hospital.

The junior nurses tittered.

Geena groaned inwardly. It was distraction enough that Valentine's Day had fallen on a Friday, a busy day in the children's ward, without some comic decorating the entire length of the front counter with chocolate kisses.

'Expecting any flowers or chocs yourself, Geena?' Petite, blonde RN Krista Logan asked cheekily.

'Cartloads,' Geena said repressively, scooping up the red foil-wrapped sweets and scattering them into an empty paper tray.

'Now, let's get the shift up and running, shall we?' Geena consulted the night sister's report, ignoring the little restive movements around her. 'You'll all have ample opportunity for play at the Valentine dance tonight.'

'Fat chance,' third-year Megan Fels said plaintively. 'I don't even have a date.'

'Just turn up on your own, then.' Krista, who seemed to have most of the answers, swept her long fringe away from her eyes. 'You never know who you might meet. Are you going, Geena?'

Geena rolled her eyes. She'd be hard pressed getting any sense out of this lot today by the sound of it. 'I don't know yet.' She had no intention of going but that was her business. 'Now, could we get on, please? We've quite a list for discharge this morning.'

Delegating duties swiftly, Geena watched her staff disperse. On the whole they were a good bunch, she acknowledged, these days looking smart and well groomed in the hospital's new uniform of navy trousers and white polo shirts.

And thank heavens for the uniform's practicality. Geena's mouth tipped into a wry smile as she took the tiny toy koala, the insignia for the children's department, and clipped it on the pocket of her shirt.

It was anyone's guess how her own day was going to shape up. Please, don't let it be too full of drama, she wished silently. She flicked open her diary.

Not bad but she had another of those interminable management meetings this afternoon. Oh, well, at least she had the weekend off…

'Morning, Geena.' Jack O'Neal, the department's SR strode into the nurses' station and propped his six-foot frame against the steel filing cabinet.

'Jack.' Geena looked up, her smile natural and warm. 'What can I do for you?'

The senior registrar's eyes narrowed marginally, before he said, 'There'll be a new admission up shortly from A and E. A two-year-old, Andrew Lynch. He was thrown against the dashboard of his mother's car this morning. She had to brake suddenly.'

Geena winced. When would parents ever learn that an unrestrained child in a car could become a missile given the wrong set of circumstances? To say nothing of it being against the law anyway to have a child under eight in the front seat. 'Much damage?'

'Don't know yet. He's in X-Ray at the moment.' Jack looked moodily into the distance. 'Samantha Greer's running a CT scan on him now. Whatever it shows, I want him admitted for observation. Obviously, we'll need to watch for any intra-cranial bleeding.'

Geena slung her pen on its cord around her neck. 'Was the mother hurt?'

A fleeting shadow crossed his face and his mouth tightened. 'Apart from shock, no. Someone's birthday?' As if seeking to change the subject entirely, Jack pushed himself away from the cabinet and helped himself to one of the valentine sweets.

Geena shook her head in disbelief. Had he actually not noticed the helium-filled red hearts that had been cluttering up the staffroom for the past two days, courtesy of the ward's social committee?

'It's Valentine's Day,' she emphasised drily.

He scoffed, lobbing the sweet wrapper into the bin. 'Surely you're not still an advocate of that old claptrap, are you?'

'What do you mean *still*?' Did he think she was past it? She might be nudging thirty but really! Geena's pique thrummed as she pulled the mountain of paperwork towards her and switched on the computer.

'A little or a lot, Jack, romance, love, caring— whatever you want to call it, it makes the world go round.'

There was a beat of silence.

'You really think so?'

'Certainly.' Geena knew her tone lacked conviction but they were talking about him here. 'And just as obviously you don't.'

He chuckled but then his smile died. 'I'm no teenager, Geena. I've been there and done that.'

Hadn't they both? Unaccountably, Geena felt her heart raise its rhythm and she frowned at the screen. 'So you've decided the whole thing isn't worth the effort, is that it?'

His mouth crimped at the corners. 'Sorry to disappoint you, Sister, but it's not something I want to remember.'

Heavens, he sounded so cynical! 'That's awful,

Jack.' Geena sucked in her bottom lip thoughtfully. 'What are you going to do about it?'

For a moment he looked startled and then he rallied. 'I'm open to suggestions.' His grin was slow and he propped his hip on the desk close to her.

Geena felt her concentration scatter like leaves in the wind as his deep blue gaze locked with hers. Awareness, like a spool of thread unravelling, began whispering down her backbone. She swallowed uncomfortably and tried to take it in. Suddenly and without warning the balance between her and Jack O'Neal had tipped, replaced by something else—something, she suspected, neither of them was prepared for.

With a barely audible click of the tongue at her wild thoughts, she swung up from the chair, collecting several patient files from the pigeon holes behind her.

'Oops! You've dropped one.' Jack stuck out a long arm and caught the file baseball-style. His mouth quirked as he held it out to her.

'Thanks.' But Geena didn't feel thankful at all. Why on earth was he still hanging about? His odd mood, the way he was looking at her, was creating havoc on her pulse rate, inciting her to feel things she didn't want to feel. Think things she didn't want to think.

'Don't you have something to do, Jack?' she asked crossly.

A teasing little grin hovered around his mouth. 'And there I was thinking I was being polite and helpful just like my mum taught me to be.'

Geena whipped her gaze away. She couldn't handle him in this mood. She didn't know what was up or down. And the heat on the back of her neck was killing her!

The phone beside them rang and Geena grabbed the receiver like a lifeline.

'It's Admin,' she mouthed at him. He nodded and, raising an eyebrow with evident amusement, wandered off towards the children's play area.

As if her eyes had a will of their own, they followed his progress, absorbing detail. Jack O'Neal was tall and rangy with a controlled kind of vitality, and with the kind of bearing that set him apart.

Geena finished her phone call and set the receiver back on its rest. What did she really know about the senior registrar anyway? she pondered. Except for the fact he was single and that they'd both arrived on the same day six months ago to work on the same ward, she knew next to nothing about his personal life.

But she did know he was wonderful with the children, co-operative with the staff and she knew, like her, he'd left one of the big teaching hospitals in Sydney to come and work in this sprawling rural city of Hopeton in central-western New South Wales.

But beyond that? Geena sighed and went back to her paperwork but Jack O'Neal's image stayed with her, overtaking reality, and she visualised his dark hair, always squeaky clean, with a tendency to spiral down onto his brow. More often than not he had a brooding look but then he'd smile and the action would chase away the broodiness, setting his eyes alight, drawing you in—

Drat the man! Geena shoved her pile of forms out of sight and went to get herself a reviving cup of coffee.

Back in his office Jack threw down the medical journal in defeat. He might as well have been reading it upside down for all he'd taken in.

Instead his thoughts kept drifting, catapulting back to Geena Wilde when he least expected it. He stifled an oath. Why now? They'd worked around one another for months now without any of this craziness happening.

He rubbed a hand across his cheekbones. The feelings of desire he'd felt had rocked him to the core and it was suddenly as though his eyes had been opened and there was Geena, not the self-sufficient charge nurse but someone else entirely.

Leaning back in his chair, he stared at the ceiling and it was as if her face were superimposed there— her hair, dark and glossy as a raven's wing around her head, her swan-like neck and straight little nose.

And her eyes—so dark they were almost black. Eyes to drown in...

'Jack?' Geena popped her head around his door, then drew back, startled. His preoccupation was almost palpable. 'I'm sorry... The door was open...'

'It's OK.' His voice was rough. He turned to her, his expression wiped clean. 'What's up?'

'I thought you'd want to see this.'

His dark brows rose interrogatively. 'Andrew's CT scan?'

'Yes.' Geena moved towards him, feeling as though she were walking in sand, ankle-deep. 'He's on the ward now. Megan is settling him in.' She placed the envelope on the desk in front of Jack.

'Fine.' Spinning off his chair, he selected the first plate and slapped it up on the viewing screen. 'I'll need to talk to the mother,' he murmured almost absently. 'This looks good.'

'She's gone,' Geena said, coming up behind him to peer over his shoulder.

'Gone?' His dark head swooped back, almost colliding with hers, and Geena made a funny little dance step to avoid a clash of heads. 'Gone where?'

'She said she had a breakfast meeting with her boss.'

Jack said something very uncomplimentary under his breath. 'Where in God's name are the woman's priorities?'

'Claudia Lynch is a sole supporting parent, Jack,'

Geena explained. 'She obviously needs her job. And apparently this boss fellow flew from Sydney this morning to meet with her.'

'So?' Jack was clearly unimpressed. 'Couldn't she have explained her son had been involved in an accident?' His face fell into sombre lines as he put the next plate up. 'The whole trauma for this child is clearly down to his mother's failure to carry out the basic safety rules for young children in cars.'

Geena gave a little shake of her head. What was eating him? He was usually so tuned in to the feelings of the parents and families. 'She's upset enough about what's happened to her son, without you jumping on her as well.'

He snorted. 'You're breaking my heart, Geena.'

'You've just finished telling me you don't believe in *hearts*,' Geena reminded him tartly.

Jack turned to her for a second, his mouth tilting slightly at the corners. 'I've really rained on your parade today, haven't I? I can see I'll have to make it up to you.'

Geena rolled her eyes heavenward and then set her gaze on the back of his handsome head.

'Look at this.' Jack drew her attention to the last of the X-rays. 'Another millimetre and who knows what the result might have been? Our little lad's been lucky.' He peeled the film off the screen.

'You still intend to admit him, though?'

'Oh, yes,' he confirmed. 'I'd prefer to err on the

side of caution and keep him in for forty-eight hours. I take it his mother is coming back?'

Geena tutted. 'Of course she is. As soon as this breakfast thing is over and done with. I spoke to her, Jack. Apparently, it was just one of those aberrations.'

Jack grunted, unconvinced.

'She was running late.' Geena opened her hands expressively. 'Andrew's care provider lives only two blocks away—'

'And she didn't take the time to restrain him properly in the back of the car.' Jack finished the little scenario, his mouth compressing into a thin line.

Geena nodded, her lashes falling in two dark half-moons to conceal her eyes.

A jagged flashback of her own childhood hit her. Her mother had been left with three small daughters to rear on her own. Geena had only to close her eyes to recall how it had been, the mad scramble every morning when the whole family had to be out the door at almost the same moment.

Geena knew it had been hard for her and her younger siblings but for her mother... Yet Geena gave her full marks for remaining determinedly cheerful throughout the battle to keep them all fed, clothed and educated. Could *she* have retained such optimism under the same circumstances?

A faint wariness clouded her eyes. She sincerely hoped she never had to find out...

'Where did you go just then?' Jack asked softly, pinning her with a questioning look.

Geena brought her head up and stared at him uncertainly, absorbing the tiny lines which framed his blue eyes, the lean angle of his jaw. She saw a face that, close up, looked faintly weathered and eyes that reserved the right to see all and reveal nothing.

'Nowhere you'd want to go,' she choked on a laugh. She felt naked inside and she looked away awkwardly. 'Did you want to see Andrew now?'

'Mmm.' Jack began to usher her from his office. 'Let's do that.'

Andrew was lying quietly in one of the large cots.

'OK?' Geena looked pointedly at Megan who was sitting by the cot, stroking the toddler's chubby little arm.

'A bit out of it, I think,' she said, getting hurriedly to her feet to make way for the registrar and charge.

'That's understandable.' Jack sent the student a smile and parked himself on the vacated chair. 'Let's see how you're doing, little mate,' he said, his movements gentle, swift and sure as he tested the child's neurological responses. 'Looking good,' he murmured, when Andrew's pupils appeared equal and reactive. Pocketing his pencil torch, he began a careful palpation of the little boy's tummy.

'Dr O'Neal is looking for any hardening that would indicate internal bleeding,' Geena explained to Megan who was doing her first block of training on the children's ward.

The student nodded. 'Andrew was examined already in A and E, though...'

'Our registrar always likes to do his own follow-up. Ssh, it's all right, baby.' Geena bent to pacify the toddler who was beginning to squirm under Jack's examination.

Megan giggled. 'Oh, look, Doctor, he wants your stethoscope.'

'No, I think he wants Rupert,' Jack contradicted her, smiling indulgently as he unclipped the tiny toy spider monkey he wore on his stethoscope and pressed it into the little boy's hand. 'Andrew, meet Rupert,' the registrar said solemnly, watching the toddler's fingers curl around the soft toy.

'Are you sure you don't mind, Dr O'Neal?' Megan bit her lip. 'We've plenty of toys he can have—'

'Yes, I'm sure.' Jack placed a hand gently against the small fair head and got to his feet. He looked across at Megan and winked. 'I've at least forty more Rupert clones in a big bag in my office,' he said with a grin.

'Oh...' Megan dipped her head and giggled.

She'd been in Kids' only a couple of weeks but she was loving it. And Jack O'Neal was to die for! She wondered if he was going to the valentine dance…

'I'll write up some pain relief for him.' Jack unclipped his pen. 'That whack he took on the forehead has probably left the poor little guy with the mother and father of a headache. And let's keep the hourly neuro obs going, please, Sister. We'll drop back to four-hourly if nothing untoward develops.'

Geena nodded. 'He's a lovely little boy, isn't he?' she said, carefully raising the rails on the cot once more. 'Well nourished and obviously cared for.'

'Mmm.' Absorbed in Andrew's chart, Jack curled his lips into a silent no-further-comment moue. He was quite aware that Geena was trying to make a point. Perhaps he had come on a bit strongly about the mother's lax attitude. Perhaps…

'OK, that's it.' He replaced the chart and pocketed his pen. 'Anyone else you'd like me to see, Sister?'

'There is, actually.' Geena swung back to give Megan some further instructions. 'By the look of it, he'll sleep soon,' she finished, bending to touch a finger to the soft little cheek. 'Oh, and, Megan, if for any reason you have to take him out of the cot, carry him. We don't want him falling.'

'Who did you need me to see?' Jack asked as

they made their way from the single room and across to one of the four-bed units.

Geena frowned. 'Jasmine Lee.'

'The little post op tonsillectomy?' Jack picked up on Geena's concern. 'What's wrong with Jassie? She was supposed to be going home this afternoon, wasn't she?'

'Well, we'd hoped so.' Geena shrugged. 'Toni Michaels declined to sign her release. And she's gone off duty now.'

'I see.' Jack's mouth firmed. If his junior resident had had concerns, he should have been informed. 'Why did no one think to call me?'

Geena sucked in her breath. 'As I recall, Doctor, you'd been paged to A and E. Even you can't be in two places at once,' she concluded drily.

'Indeed.' He threw her a wry grin. 'Superman I'm not. It's probably just a glitch with Jassie anyway.'

Preceding him into the unit, Geena felt that odd tingling down her backbone again. Like the brush of his fingers. She was appalled. Fascinated.

She swallowed the lump that had suddenly appeared in her throat and handed him Jasmine's notes.

As it turned out, the child had an elevated temperature. That wasn't a problem in itself but could perhaps be the forerunner of something else.

'We'll try her on some liquid Panadol for the

temp.' Jack glanced at the rest of the notes. 'OK.' He handed them back to Geena. 'Let's have a look at you, Jassie.' Smiling at the solemn little three-year-old, he began talking to her gently, taking all the time in the world to reassure her.

'Nothing's obviously presenting itself,' he concluded after his careful examination, 'but I'd like to run some blood tests, get some cultures and see if that turns up anything.'

'Mrs Lee's just getting a coffee in the parents' lounge,' Geena said quietly. 'I think she'd like a word.'

'No problem.' Jack glanced at his watch. 'After that, I'll be at Mercy for a consult with Derek Chalmers. I may be a while but if you need me, just ring.'

After he'd gone, Geena felt her heart struggle back into its rightful place. Sighing, she swept an impatient hand through her softly layered hair. What was going on here? She felt as though the whole of her equilibrium had been stood on its head, shaken and put back in all the wrong places.

The reason—Jack O'Neal. The remedy? She wished she knew.

In the whole of her adult life she'd had only one serious love affair, George Cominos. Her smile became faintly cynical. He'd been an intern and she'd been in the final weeks of her nurse's training.

The time they'd spent together had been special

but that hadn't stopped him dropping her smartly as soon as he'd got the opportunity to work at a state-of-the-art private hospital interstate.

Trusting and largely inexperienced with men, she'd offered to join him as soon as she'd acquired her sister's stripes, but she'd been met with embarrassment and awkward words. He wanted out of their relationship and it seemed her feelings had no part in his decision.

Thinking back, she was suddenly jolted into a reappraisal of her attitude at the time. With hindsight, perhaps she'd been too intense, hellbent on using George's affection to fill the lonely gaps...

She clicked her tongue and shook her head as if to clear it. What was the point of wallowing in the past like this? She had a busy ward to run. And Jack's odd behaviour and how it was affecting her to contend with.

CHAPTER TWO

SOMEONE'S out to get me. The thought provoked Geena into a humourless laugh.

The ward phone had rung incessantly, her paperwork remained largely untouched and she had only a sketchy kind of report ready for the management meeting.

On the positive side Jasmine's temperature had begun to come down and Geena was hopeful Jack would allow the little poppet to go home. The results of the bloods wouldn't be known for a few days and if it proved necessary, Jassie could be followed up at one of his regular clinics.

Now for a word with Andrew's mother. Geena was quietly pleased. Her instincts had been right. Claudia Lynch was no neglectful mother. She'd got back to the hospital as soon as she could and was now spending time with her son.

She was sitting in the big recliner chair when Geena walked in. 'Oh, Sister—' Claudia looked up startled. 'He's just woken up.'

'That's lovely.' Geena smiled and checked Andrew's chart. 'He's doing really well, aren't you, little one? Would you like to cuddle him for a while?'

'Could I?' The young woman seemed pathetically grateful, scooping herself out of the chair and moving to the side of the cot.

'Come on, young man.' Deftly Geena lifted Andrew and handed him over to his mother.

'My boss told me to take whatever time I needed.' Claudia pressed her fair head close to her son's.

Geena nodded. 'That must have been a great relief for you.' She picked up the cot blanket and refolded it. 'You can stay with him tonight as well, if you'd like to.'

'I'd love to.' Claudia's arms tightened around the toddler. 'Will I be allowed to help with his care?'

'Wherever possible.' Geena's tone was gentle. 'We'll keep Andrew rather quiet today on account of the bump on his head. But you could give him a little change of scene later. Carry him about the ward for a bit.'

Claudia nodded. 'Will he be able to eat something?'

The simple little question wrung Geena's heart. She looked at the tiny hand curled so trustingly against his mother. They looked so right together. So interlinked. Parent and child.

'He'll be on clear fluids only today.' Geena forced back the odd tightening in her stomach. 'And if he has a good night, we'll review his care again first thing.'

Claudia bit her lip then lifted her head. 'Thanks for explaining everything. Could I…talk to you again about some other stuff?'

'That's what we're here for.' Geena unfurled one of her special smiles, sensing this young mum's burning need for a simple, old-fashioned heart-to-heart. 'I'll make time later on,' she said.

Although heaven knew when, she thought ruefully, making her way through the play area to the ward kitchen. A swift glance at her watch indicated it was morning teatime already.

'Everything OK?' Geena popped her head through the big sliding window which connected the play area to the kitchen. Several of the staff were busily preparing drinks and snacks for their young patients.

'It's a zoo in here today,' Krista complained. 'That kid, Aiden Luft, is being a real toad.'

'He's testing you, ducky,' Brenda Hearn, the mature-age enrolled nurse said kindly. 'He's bored.'

'He's a boy!' Krista countered darkly, taking a large jug of milk from the fridge and setting it on the counter top with a little thump.

'What's he done this time?' Automatically, Geena picked up the jug and began to fill the plastic beakers with chocolate-flavoured milk. Twelve-year-old Aiden had cystic fibrosis and was in hospital for his usual maintenance programme.

Krista shot the charge an exasperated look. 'Only

hid a vital piece from each of the jigsaws, which sent all the little kids crazy.'

Geena bit back a smile. Aiden was clearly frustrated and perhaps in his own way trying to prove his point—that he was too old to be in the children's ward at all. 'Surely he should have been doing his school lessons?'

'He was for a while,' Brenda put in. 'Then he told Mrs French he didn't feel up to it. You know what a softie she is.'

'Hey, people!' Piers Korda, Geena's deputy and the only male RN in the department, strolled in and helped himself to several of the crackers Krista was preparing for the children's snacks.

'Shove off!' Krista slapped his hand. 'Doesn't your wife feed you?'

'Not lately.' His mouth turned down comically.

Geena sent him a sympathetic smile. 'How is Tasha?'

'Improving, I think.' He looked at Geena through the dividing window, his eyes full of weary good humour. 'At least the morning sickness is down to a dull roar. And your bright idea that I stagger my starting times for work has made a hell of a difference.'

'Are you and Tasha coming to the dance?' Krista, who was on the social committee, asked hopefully.

'Don't think we're up to dancing, Kris.' Piers shook his head. 'Sorry.'

Krista sighed extravagantly. 'I don't think anyone's coming!'

'Rubbish!' Brenda waved a dismissive hand. 'The folk from A and E always come.'

'And scoff all the finger food before the rest of us get a look in,' Piers said drily.

'Well, some of them have to get back on duty,' Brenda said fairly. 'And they all buy tickets whether they can stay or not.'

Geena chuckled. She'd been at the hospital only six months and had no idea what went on at the valentine dance, but it sounded like it could be fun. She made a little pattern on the counter top with her finger. Perhaps she should change her mind. Think about going…

'Geena, these just came for you.' Diane Lewis, the ward receptionist, held out a sheaf of long-stemmed roses. Laughing softly, she made a little mock curtsy. 'Aren't you the lucky one?'

'For me?' Geena jumped guiltily. She'd been miles away from her responsibilities as charge.

'Red roses…' There was a collective sigh.

Her colour high, Geena bit her lip, looking down helplessly at the flowers she now held in her arms.

'They're old-fashioned garden roses!' someone exclaimed. 'Smell the perfume.'

'Probably came from that new shop in the arcade,' Brenda speculated practically. 'What's it called? Bibs and Bobs?'

'Bouquets and Blossoms,' Krista corrected with a giggle. 'Aren't they just gorgeous?' Leaning across the counter, she touched a fingertip to one of the petals. 'Darren only gave me a mixed bunch from Woolworths.' She made a pretty little pout.

'Lucky you!' Diane snorted. 'I didn't even get a Mars bar from Gary.'

More laughter.

A bit choked, her eyes prickling, Geena heard the good-natured banter going on around her. She couldn't remember the last time she'd received flowers...

'Well, who are they from, Geena?'

'Is there a card?'

Geena heard the excited questions, saw the expectant faces and made a supreme effort at composure. 'Yes, there is,' she said brightly. With a flick of her wrist she detached the florist's white envelope and glanced at her name spelled out in the familiar firm handwriting. She swallowed. What did Jack O'Neal think he was playing at?

'Well?' Krista's impatience erupted in a shriek. 'Who sent them?'

'No one.' Blinking, Geena hastily shoved the card into the side pocket of her trousers.

'Spoilsport,' someone else grumbled.

Her heart pounding, Geena looked around in confusion.

'Why don't I grab some vases for these beauties?' Piers materialised beside her, his brown gaze kind.

'Oh, would you, Piers? Thanks.' Almost throwing the roses into his waiting arms, Geena fled.

In the privacy of her office and with the door firmly closed, she reread the note.

'Lunch in the park. Twelve o'clock. I'll wait near the bush chapel.'

The arrogance of the man! Geena gnawed on her bottom lip. Fancy not even bothering to sign it! But, then, why would he? He knew she was familiar with his handwriting. She saw it a dozen times a day.

The speed with which he'd moved sent her heart fluttering in alarm. A wave of sheer panic hollowed out her insides, yet her body felt more alive than it had for an age.

Crossing to the window, she looked out. Hopeton's beautiful memorial park was situated directly opposite the hospital grounds. Geena had walked through it often, knew exactly where Jack O'Neal would be waiting...

An hour later Geena took a calming breath. Suddenly, twelve o'clock seemed so close.

Oh, really! She bit back a self-derisive laugh. Anyone would think she was nineteen instead of twenty-nine but if she was honest, this date with Jack was making her as shy as a schoolgirl.

What of him? Determinedly she tapped in the final paragraph of her report and checked the spelling. He was probably just out for a lark, a one-off diversion because she'd made such a fuss about it being Valentine's Day.

She made a little huff of annoyance. Why on earth hadn't she kept her mouth closed and her opinions to herself—?

'I've had a chat to young Aiden,' Piers said from the region of her shoulder. 'Man to man.'

Geena turned her head and blinked. 'Oh, good.' She smiled. 'Got him occupied elsewhere, have you?'

'Mmm.' Piers' mouth crooked into a grin. 'Folding nappies.'

Geena got a mental picture and chuckled.

'Mind you, I had to agree to let him play one of his mindless video games later,' Piers admitted ruefully. 'But for the moment peace reigns in the littlies play room.'

'Well done,' Geena approved softly, looking at the rather rugged face of her deputy. He was such a nice man, she thought. No wonder his wife was dotty about him.

'Piers...' Geena swallowed. It was now or never. 'I'd like to take the early lunch today. Could you cover?'

'No worries,' he responded cheerfully. 'Got a lunch date, have you?'

'Oh, no,' Geena felt the heat in her cheeks and tried to look away. 'Not really.'

Piers's eyes softened. 'The sender of the red roses, one presumes?'

'I suppose I'm the talk of the whole department?' With her head bent, Geena gathered her copies together.

'Think of your street cred.' Piers' grin was infectious. 'Probably sky high by now.'

Street cred be damned! Her cheeks burning, Geena held her papers to her chest and wished Jack O'Neal to the back of beyond.

'Actually, I wanted a word with the reg.' Piers was suddenly back in his professional role. 'Is he about?'

'Jack?' Geena bit hard on her bottom lip. It was all getting so complicated. 'Probably still over at Mercy.'

'Not to worry.' Piers began to move away. 'It'll keep. Oh, Geena...' He turned back, knuckling his forehead. 'We've a hiccup with Breanna Strickland's IV.'

Geena frowned. 'It'll need resiting shortly.'

'Mmm. But her dad's just rung. As you know, he's the only one who can get her to co-operate.' Piers's mouth turned down. 'Mr Strickland can't get here until later and Breanna will create blue murder if we try to do any procedure without him present.'

'Poor little kid.' Geena shook her head. 'Probably best if we wait, then,' she went on cautiously. 'It won't make a great deal of difference in the long term and far better not to upset her needlessly.' She shot her deputy a dry smile. 'A job for Megan, I think. Get her to read Breanna some stories, jolly her along until Mr Strickland gets here.'

'Will do.' Piers spread his hands across the back of the chair. 'I'll explain what's happening to the child as well. For a five-year-old she's a very smart little cookie. She doesn't miss a beat.'

Geena glanced down at her papers. 'Well, the antibiotic seems to be doing its work. She should be home by early next week. One bush picnic that family won't forget, I'm sure.'

'Lucky they sought medical attention as early as they did,' Piers concluded. 'Untreated, that wound could have had far more serious consequences.'

Geena glanced down at her watch and Piers took the hint. 'Enjoy your lunch,' he said, his wink huge and conspiratorial. 'And don't hurry back. We'll cope.'

She only hoped *she* could. Geena watched him go and then went back to her office. She looked at her watch again, conscious the nerves in her stomach were doing a weird kind of dance of their own.

Even the very first day of her training hadn't been as nerve-racking as this, she decided grimly.

At ten minutes to twelve she knew she couldn't pretend any longer. Like it or not, she had an invitation to lunch. Opening the lower drawer of her desk, she pulled out her small make-up bag.

'Well, that's the best I can do at short notice,' she told her reflection wryly a few minutes later. Lifting a hand, she flicked open the second button on her shirt then just as quickly refastened it.

A welter of unfamiliar emotions engulfed her as she quietly left her office and made her way to the stairwell. No way she was going to risk bumping into anyone in the lift and fuelling any further speculation.

Despite the oddness of her mood, Geena drew in a pleasurable breath as she crossed the road to the park, acknowledging it was easy to forget the existence of the outside world when you were cocooned within the precincts of the hospital for most of the day.

And such a beautiful day too, she thought, stepping past the drooping foliage of a huge old pepper tree and on to the lawn beyond.

Continuing on, she walked swiftly along the path flanked by deciduous liquidambars, their summertime leaves green and crisp. It was hard to imagine that, come autumn, these same leaves would, almost overnight, turn to stunning golds and reds.

Lifting her head, Geena caught the tantalising smell of woodsmoke, resolving then and there to try to get out more often for her lunch break.

The bush chapel was set in a clearing, delineated simply by a semicircle of park benches and a stone-sculptured cross.

Geena saw Jack waiting and something seemed to melt in her stomach. He was sitting on the bench with his back against the picnic table, his long legs stretched out in front of him.

Jack looked up, seeing her coming towards him. He felt sick, seriously doubting his sanity over this whole Valentine's Day hype. More to the point, he was beginning to doubt his own readiness for what amounted to a date with Geena Wilde. Well, it was too late now to renege. She was already here...

He schooled his facial muscles into a smile and pushed himself to his feet. 'You came,' he said, cringing inwardly at the inanity of the greeting.

'What did you expect me to do, Jack?' Geena drew to a rather breathless stop in front of him. 'Surely you didn't think I'd ignore your invitation?'

He laughed softly, suddenly feeling absurdly young and more hopeful than he had in years. 'I'd hoped you wouldn't.'

A rush of uncertainty claimed Geena and she felt cut off from reality, swimming wildly in uncharted seas. She swallowed drily. 'The roses were lovely. Thanks.'

His mouth curved into a wry smile. 'I wish I could have been there to see your face.'

Geena's dark lashes swooped down, hiding the vulnerability in her eyes. 'You can be sure everyone else did,' she informed him. 'I take it this is our picnic?' She gestured towards the cane basket on the table beside them.

'Mmm.' Jack removed the red-checked paper tablecloth with a flourish. 'Courtesy of Jamiesons.'

Geena's brows lifted. Nothing but the best.

'I was really amazed to find such an upmarket deli outside of Sydney,' she confessed, eagerly lifting out the assorted goodies and placing them on the cloth.

'Jamiesons have been here for ever,' Jack said dismissively. 'In fact, I had a Saturday job with them during my final year of high school.'

Geena was taken aback. She'd assumed that, like her, he was city born and bred. 'So, you've really come home?'

'In a manner of speaking.' He supplied the comment casually, flipping open a carton of fruit juice and pouring them each a measure. 'The O'Neals have lived in the district for three generations.'

'And you have an old family home?' Geena was intrigued, impressed. She'd known nothing more substantial than a series of flats for the whole of her life.

Jack shrugged. 'The family had a property originally—Wongaree. It was about a thousand hectares. It's been sold off now except for twenty-five which includes the homestead.'

'And that's where you live?' Geena looked slightly bewildered.

'I bought it from my parents when they retired up the coast. I hated to think of the whole place being lost to future generations,' he admitted with a rueful half-smile. 'I'm the oldest of five. None of the others had any desire for a life in the country—except Belinda,' he added as an afterthought. 'She's a flight attendant for Qantas. She wanders up here occasionally for a bit of R and R.' He stopped and gave a dry laugh. 'Listen to me rabbiting on. Sorry...'

'You haven't,' Geena shook her head. 'It's interesting.'

'Your drink.' Jack held out the frosted glass of juice towards her. 'Ideally, I guess we should be drinking wine.'

'But not when we're both on duty.' Geena smothered a laugh. 'Wouldn't be a good image, would it? Senior Reg and Charge drunk and disorderly on duty.'

Jack looked at her bent head, the soft curve of her cheek, the sweet fullness of her mouth... 'I can't imagine you being either,' he observed, a small twist to his smile.

'No.' Geena shook her dark head. 'That's not me

at all. Mmm…' She changed tack quickly. 'All this looks wonderful.' She looked up into those blue, blue eyes. 'Hungry?'

Oh, yes, he was hungry all right. He was hungry for the company of a woman. A woman who was special, caring. And Geena Wilde seemed to fit the bill on both counts. Jack took a steadying breath, one that took in her faint, delicate fragrance…

'Geena?'

'Hmm?' She looked up from placing food on the disposable picnic plates.

'Nothing…' Jack shook his head as if to clear it. He gave a cracked laugh. 'I'm starved.'

'Me too.' Geena's dark eyes tracked over his face for a moment and then she looked away, biting her lip. Oh, Lord. There was enough undercurrent here to drown them. Her pulse raced at the thought of being caught up in a wild, passionate encounter with Jack O'Neal.

What utter rubbish, she thought and gave her collar a little straightening twist. 'Come on, then.' She used her most rallying tone. 'Let's try to do justice to this beautiful food, shall we?'

The food was indeed wonderful. There were crusty bread rolls, tiny succulent tomatoes, a smoky-tasting rich Cheddar, curls of finely cut leg ham and a potato salad that was just begging to be eaten and enjoyed.

'This stuff is delicious,' Geena said, forking up a second helping.

'It's Mira Jamieson's speciality.' Jack placed a dab of tangy relish on the side of his plate. 'She's Italian-born,' he explained. 'I recall her telling me the recipe came from southern Italy.'

'Hence the olives.' Geena cleaned her plate and leaned back with the sigh. 'That was fantastic, Jack. Thank you. I won't eat for another week,' she groaned laughingly.

'Do you have to hurry back?' He began gathering up their plates and stacking them to one side.

'I suppose not.' Geena gave a shrug. 'Piers is covering for me.'

'And Phil Carter is covering for me.' Jack reached into the basket and produced a small Thermos flask. He uncorked it and poured them each a mug of the steaming, aromatic brew. 'Can you fit in a coffee?' he asked with a grin.

'Just about.' Geena cocked a wry eyebrow. 'It smells divine and you've thought of everything. I can't remember the last time I—' She stopped and dipped her head defensively. 'Well, as I said, it's been wonderful.'

'For me too,' Jack said quietly, and realised with some amazement it was true. Then he discovered another amazing thing. From having firmly decided that wild horses wouldn't drag him to the valentine dance, he found himself inviting Geena to accompany him.

'I hadn't actually made up my mind whether to go or not.' She hesitated. 'I bought a book of their raffle tickets, though.'

He grinned sheepishly. 'I bought six.'

'Show-off!' Geena wrinkled her nose, lifting her mug to take a mouthful of her coffee. Her heart was thrumming and she felt that if she tried to get up and walk, her feet wouldn't even begin to touch the ground. 'Apparently a hefty part of the profits goes towards replacing toys and equipment for our department,' she said reflectively.

'Then we should go.' Jack was definite. 'I'll pick you up about nine. I can't make it any earlier, I'm afraid. I probably won't get out of the hospital until sevenish and I have animals to feed when I get home.'

'Animals?' Geena raised an eyebrow. How many did he have, for goodness' sake? 'What? Dogs? Cats?'

'No,' he laughed. 'Australian natives mostly. I help the wildlife association where I can. Some of the animals have been mauled by dogs and have to be merely kept quiet until they heal. Others are poorly for various reasons.'

Geena shook her head, chuckling. 'Are you a frustrated vet, Jack?'

'Ah!' He grinned, showing even white teeth.

'That, as they say, is a story for another time.' Raising his arms to half-mast, he began to stretch leisurely.

Geena blinked, her gaze helplessly entrapped. He flexed his limbs slowly, rhythmically, the rolled-up sleeves of his blue striped Oxford shirt revealing his tanned forearms, their dusting of hair gleaming almost golden in the sunlight.

Geena suppressed a shiver, her hands clenching around her coffee-mug. What was the matter with her? Good grief! She'd seen his bare arms before. He was in and out of the ward in Theatre scrubs a dozen times a week.

So what had happened? Had some fundamental change taken place within herself? And why suddenly today did everything about him, about his body, seem to call to her?

You're daft! Admonishing herself silently, she stood quickly and began to shake the crumbs from the tablecloth. 'Here, birds,' she called, watching several native jabiru, their bright red legs looking almost too fragile to carry them, begin to pick their way daintily towards her.

'What a very sweet scene,' Jack murmured, his hand coming down to rest lightly on her shoulder.

'The birds?' Geena gave an uncertain little laugh. 'And you...'

'Oh.' She hastily folded the tablecloth, feeling as though her legs had turned to jelly, as though his touch—the mere sensation of it—had inundated her whole body.

She swallowed. 'Jack...'

'Don't talk.' Gently, he turned her to face him. The touch of his fingers was like thistledown as he lifted her chin so that he could stare silently into her eyes, before he lowered his mouth to hers.

The tablecloth dropped from Geena's nerveless fingers and a pain, sweet and piercing, flooded her being. She felt his mouth, gentle, searching, tender. It felt so right, tasted like nectar. While he held her mouth his fingers caressed her cheek, the tip of his thumb stroking her jaw.

Geena felt as if her bones were melting. Her hands reached out tentatively—went to his waist, higher to the nubs of his shoulder blades, higher still to the strong column of his neck. Her fingers parted, weaving through the softness of the hair at his nape.

Jack's hand tightened on her shoulder for a moment before he released her mouth and drew back, ever so slowly.

'So...' His voice came out huskily uneven. Spreading his fingers along the side of her throat, he said her name softly, so softly.

Geena shivered.

'You OK?' He brushed a kiss across her temple.

She nodded. She was—just. She could still taste him and the tender passion of his kiss.

They packed up the remains of their picnic in silence. Geena felt shaken beyond belief, all thumbs.

What happens now? she wondered, and her heart gave a sideways lerch.

What do you want to happen now? a little inner voice tantalised her.

CHAPTER THREE

GEENA frowned. 'Hear that?'

'What?' Jack's head spun up and they both listened. 'Sounds like someone's in trouble—over there!' He pointed towards the neatly clipped high hedge. 'Come on!' He grabbed Geena's hand and they began running.

Oh, God! Geena felt a stitch in her side. She bit her lips. She should never have had that second helping of potato salad!

'Over here!' Jack wheeled sharply and Geena immediately saw the young woman, almost staggering under the weight of quite a large child.

'What's happened?' Automatically, Jack took the child and held her.

The young mother shook her head and gulped.

'What happened?' Jack snapped. 'Tell me! I'm a doctor!'

'I need the hospital… Oh, please!' The woman's hand went to her throat. 'She can't seem to breathe properly. It just happened— I don't—'

'Jack!' Geena's keen eyes caught the red weal of a beesting on the child's upper arm. The little girl was wearing a simple, vest-like T-shirt, her tender skin exposed.

'Come on, baby...' Jack breathed, his fingers seeking a pulse in the little girl's neck. His mouth drew in. The pulse was there—just. They still had time. He swung around. 'Follow me!' he snapped, and began running.

'But...' The young woman looked wildly around, the tattered remains of a kite dangling from her hand.

'I'll take you across to the hospital.' Geena put a guiding hand on the woman's arm. 'It looks like your little one has had a beesting,' she explained, hurrying the distracted parent through a small gap in the hedge. 'She's obviously allergic to the venom.'

'Oh, my God...'

The mother's little sob tore at Geena's heart. 'It'll be all right,' she soothed, mentally crossing her fingers.

'What will they do?' The young woman clutched distractedly at Geena's arm.

'They'll give her adrenalin.' With her outstretched hand, Geena collected the picnic basket as they sped past the table she and Jack had used. 'It'll work very swiftly to counteract the venom in your daughter's body.'

The woman gulped. 'They—won't have to do one of those tracky things, will they?'

'Tracheostomy.' Geena was calmly reassuring. 'Let's hope it won't be necessary.'

'What if it happens again?' The mother, who'd introduced herself as Jeanette McIntyre, asked anxiously.

'There are desensitisation injections available now.' Geena put a guiding hand on the woman's arm as they crossed the road back to the hospital. 'I'm sure Dr O'Neal will advise whether they'll be suitable for your little one.'

Jeanette looked stricken. 'My poor little Katie... It was my day off. We came to the park for a treat.'

'You weren't to know,' Geena said soothingly. 'Just be thankful you were so near the hospital.'

When they arrived at the entrance of A and E, Geena whisked the young mother inside. 'Just wait here,' she said kindly. 'I'll find out what's happening with Katie.' Geena had already spotted Cassie Gordon, one of the department's senior nurses, at the station.

'Looking for the wolf, Red Riding Hood?' Cassie greeted her contemporary with a grin, pointing to the picnic basket still clutched in Geena's hand.

'Very droll!' Geena rolled her eyes and shoved the offending basket out of sight behind the counter. 'Actually, I'm looking for Jack O'Neal.'

'Same thing,' Cassie snickered. 'Lean and hungry.' She sobered. 'I'm just back from lunch but I think I saw him disappear into cube four. What's up?'

'Child with a suspected allergic reaction. Bee-sting probably.'

'Oh, poor mite.' Cassie sent a sideways nod towards the entrance. 'Is that the parent over there?'

'Mmm.' Geena straightened away from the counter. 'Jeanette McIntyre, and the child is Kate.'

'I'll sort her out,' the sister said cheerfully. 'Oh, and Geena?'

'Yes?'

'Nice one.'

'Sorry?'

'You and Jack.'

Geena stifled a groan and waved a dismissive hand. She went to find Jack, quite convinced that, courtesy of the hospital grapevine, they'd no doubt be listed as an item by mid-afternoon.

Pulling back the curtain, Geena went into the emergency room. 'How is she?' she asked softly of Jack.

'Responding,' he said, his hand still holding the oxygen mask over the child's face.

Geena nodded. They'd certainly worked fast. Already the drip was up, sending the venom-combating drug into Kate's little veins.

'Piece of luck you were both in the park when it happened.' Mary Duffy, the SR, smiled warmly at Geena. 'Could have been a very different outcome.'

'Yes, it could.' Geena dropped her gaze to the drowsy child, noticing that her little mouth and eyes were still uncomfortably swollen. 'I managed to get a name, too,' she said quietly. 'It's Kate McIntyre. And the mum's outside, Mary. Cassie's getting details.'

'Excellent.' Mary unclipped her pen and prepared to record their treatment of the child. 'It's your call, Jack,' she said calmly. 'What do you want to do about this infant?'

Jack scraped a hand across his jaw. 'I'd like to admit her so we can keep an eye on her for the next forty-eight hours.' He directed a glance at Geena. 'We'll move her upstairs as soon as it's feasible.'

'Right.' Geena moved towards the doorway. 'I'll get back and arrange a bed. I imagine the mother could do with a cup of tea and a sit-down as well.'

On the way back to her ward, Geena glanced at her watch and sighed. It felt like she'd been gone for hours when, in reality, she was scarcely over her allotted break.

Detailing Brenda to make up a bed for Kate, she slipped back to her office.

She sat in her chair, deep in thought for a moment, and then she bent and opened a drawer in her desk.

Peering into the tiny make-up mirror, she studied her face. For what? she wondered with a little spurt of irritation. Signs she'd been kissed? And there were, she admitted reluctantly. Her mouth looked fuller somehow, softer...

She dragged in a shaky breath, picking up the phone as it rang beside her.

'Hi, it's me,' Cassie said. 'Your patient is on the way up.'

'Thanks Cass.' Geena quickly scooped up her make-up bag and stowed it out of sight as someone knocked.

'Got a minute?' Piers poked his head in.

Geena beckoned him in.

'There's room for two more at our table tonight,' Cassie drawled. 'Interested?'

'I don't know...' Geena swallowed. 'Sit down,' she mouthed at her deputy.

'Jack is,' Cassie chuckled.

Geena felt her cheeks flame. Heavens, were she and Jack wearing labels or something? She looked up and saw Piers's eyes bright with interest and all but ground her teeth. 'Whatever, then, Cass.' She hoped she'd managed to sound sufficiently non-committal. 'See you tonight.'

'Going to the dance?' Piers spread his large hands on the desktop in front of him.

'Looks like it.' Geena shrugged.

Piers's dark brows went up. 'You don't sound too thrilled about it?'

Geena began straightening things on her desk. 'I...just feel suddenly on show...' She bit her lip. 'Jack's asked me to go with him,' she confessed, feeling her stomach turn upside down again.

'It was only a matter of time, Geena.' Piers looked pleased. 'You look absolutely right together.'

'Do we indeed?' Geena gave a stilted laugh. 'Fancy that!'

Piers's mouth crimped at the corners. 'You just might have fun, you know?'

'Mmm...' Geena looked wry, clipping her pen back around her neck. 'Now, what did you want to see me about?' she asked, scraping up her professionalism as she looked enquiringly across at her deputy.

'We're being sent a suspected pertussis. Eight-year-old boy. Referral from one of the GPs.'

'Not immunised, I take it?'

Piers leaned back in his chair, hitching one leg across his knee. 'Apparently not. Parents don't believe in it—or didn't. Bet they wish now they'd had him done,' he added grimly.

Geena shook her head and thought of the implications of what was more commonly known as whooping cough.

'It can be extremely debilitating,' Geena agreed, thinking of the awful coughing fits that usually accompanied the illness.

'And contagious as all hell.' Piers looked a bit grim. 'Brenda's offered to be responsible for the boy's initial care.'

Kind, motherly Brenda would, Geena thought

gratefully. She got to her feet. 'We'll need to set up a bed in Isolation.'

'All done,' Piers said, jackknifing upright. He looked thoughtful. 'You know, Geena, it's a distinct possibility the younger members of staff would not have seen a case of whooping cough.'

'Would you have a chat to them?' Geena followed her deputy outside. 'Perhaps it'll be a one-off?'

Piers grunted. 'Don't hold your breath. The last time I had reason to check our inoculation rate, I found it was way below optimum levels.'

'Oh, Lord...' Geena shook her head.

'It could possibly be a long haul for this little chap,' Piers predicted gravely. 'And quite unnecessary if his parents had done the right thing.'

'Except, perhaps, they considered they *were* doing the right thing,' Geena summed up quietly.

'Could I possibly ring my husband?' Jeanette McIntyre had seen her daughter settled in the ward and now turned diffidently to Geena.

'Of course you can.' Geena smiled. 'Use my office.'

'Don works in a factory,' Jeanette explained. 'He won't be able to come to the phone but I could probably leave a message for him to ring me here.'

'Do that,' Geena said. 'If he asks for the children's ward, someone will find you.'

'I can't thank you enough—you and Dr O'Neal.' Jeanette wound her thin arms around her midriff. 'He's just lovely, isn't he?'

Geena's lashes flew up, exposing eyes that still held the sheen of vulnerability. 'Yes.' She swallowed. 'He's very good with the children. Here we are.' Her tone was suddenly brisk and she opened the door of her office. 'I think you'll find everything you need. Give me a shout when you're through. We'll organise a cup of tea.'

Closing the door, Geena made her way back to the station. She made a little click of exasperation. She'd have to pull herself together. Good grief! She couldn't start dissolving into self-consciousness every time Jack's name was mentioned!

Jack was already at the nurses' station, parked against the counter, his head bent over a patient's file.

'Hi,' Geena said, her clenched hand resisting the urge to reach out and pluck the unruly lock of hair off his forehead.

'Hi, yourself.' He didn't look up. 'What's the latest on our pertussis?'

'He should be here soon,' Geena responded quietly. 'William Townsend, parents John and Tiffany.'

'I've had a word with Admissions.' With a warm smile, Jack returned the file to the ward clerk. 'I figure the sooner we get the child through the red tape and receiving some kind of treatment the better.' He shot Geena a quizzical blue glance. 'Have you had time to assess our own staff's immunity situation?'

'Piers has already had a word with them,' Geena confirmed. 'We're OK but I've left instructions that any of William's visitors who are uncertain about their status will need to gown and mask.'

Jack folded his arms, his lean jaw swivelling to an angle. 'Derek tells me they have a case over at Mercy as well. Parents need their backsides kicked for neglecting this basic part of their children's health care,' he growled.

'Except for some of them, it's a calculated choice,' Geena pointed out diplomatically.

Jack snorted. 'What choice did these kids have, when they're now suffering from a disease that was preventable in the first place?'

'Jack...' Geena touched his arm. 'That looks like the Townsends now.'

The lift had disgorged a trolley carrying a child with the two people, obviously the parents, following closely behind.

As they moved to meet the group, Geena was aware that Piers had materialised quietly beside her and Brenda had gone forward to take the trolley from the accompanying aide.

Taking one look at the parents' faces, Jack frowned. This could be a bit sticky, he decided, and put out his hand. 'Mr and Mrs Townsend? I'm Jack O'Neal, the senior registrar.'

'We don't need a lecture from any of you!' Blotchy patches of red stood out on Tiffany Townsend's pale cheeks and Jack's hand was ignored.

'Tiff...' John Townsend placed his arm awkwardly around his wife's shoulders. He gave the group an apologetic grimace.

'We're not here to give anyone lectures, Mrs Townsend.' Jack straightened to his full six feet. 'We're here to make William comfortable and, hopefully, well again.'

The pale blue of the mother's eyes dissolved in a shimmer of tears. 'The GP treated us like *poison*.'

Geena could see Jack's tight-lipped expression as he turned to her. 'Sister, if you wouldn't mind? We'll need a history.'

Quietly, Geena delegated to her deputy, knowing he was skilled at his job and had enough nous to sort out the parents without getting their backs up any further than they already were.

She favoured the Townsends with one of her special smiles. 'Would you go with Nurse Korda now, please? We'll look after William and you can see him when he's settled in.'

Jack muttered under his breath as they watched the couple follow Piers, Mrs Townsend dabbing at her eyes with the large handkerchief her husband had handed her. 'What brought all that on?'

Geena shrugged, her mouth faintly set. 'Guilt, most probably,' she sighed.

With calm good humour, Brenda had settled William into the isolation room and got him ready for Jack's initial examination.

'How are you feeling, old mate?' The SR's face was set in concentration as he flicked his stethoscope over the boy's chest.

'My tummy hurts...' the little lad whispered. His fair head went back on the pillow and he began a paroxysm of coughing.

Jack looked grim as he completed his examination and pocketed his stethoscope. 'Let's get him on a nebuliser stat, please, Sister. We'll need the usual bronchodilators.'

Geena nodded. Her mind leaping ahead, she'd begun to prepare an IV. With the continual coughing ending more often than not in vomiting, the child was rapidly becoming dehydrated.

'Good work.' Jack looked on approvingly. 'Go with normal saline. And would you order some chest pysio as well, please?'

'What drugs will you treat him with?' Geena gently tipped William's head and got the nebuliser into place. 'Come on, honey,' she said, letting her hand rest on his soft hair for a moment. 'Just breathe away. Good boy.'

'I'll try him on tetracyclines.' Jack was busily writing on William's chart. 'That seems to be the consensus in paeds at the moment.'

Geena's feet hardly touched the ground for the remainder of the shift. At least she'd got in and out of her meeting in record time, she thought thankfully. And William had begun to settle nicely.

He'd been exhausted, poor little pet. But, then, so had his parents. Her mouth folded into a wry smile. Thanks mostly to Piers, their self-esteem had been somewhat restored. Piers had poured on the tea and sympathy and persuaded them to go home and get a good night's rest.

She pushed through the door into the empty staffroom and helped herself to a cup of coffee. Taking a slow mouthful, she moved across to the window that looked down on a tangle of ivy-walled garden where a beam of sunlight had pried its way through a chink in the bricks to illuminate the silver-green leaves.

Jack swung open the door and saw her standing there, the sight of her, so vulnerably feminine, starting his heart beating in a way it hadn't for years.

'How's the coffee?' He shot a hand through his hair.

'On its last legs.' Geena gave a faint grimace. 'But at least it's hot.'

He pretended to shudder. 'I think I'll be kind to

my body and stick to water. I'm about to release Aiden,' he went on, moving across to the cooler. 'Want to come and tell him the good news?'

'The weekend shift will bless you for that.' She emptied the dregs of her coffee into the sink. 'Our Aiden is a bit of a handful.'

Jack shrugged. 'There seems little point in prolonging his stay. I'm happy with his present pancreatic enzyme replacement and his parents are very tuned in to his fitness programme.' He took several mouthfuls of water. 'All things considered, I thought I'd let him go.'

They found Aiden in the play room. He was looking thoroughly fed up.

'How's it going, sport?' Jack dropped onto the lounge beside him.

Aiden shrugged.

'Not too much interesting on the telly, hmm?'

'It's boring kids' stuff.'

Jack pursed his lips and watched the boy for a moment. 'How would you like to go home?'

Hope flared in the youngster's eyes. 'Like when? Tomorrow?'

'What about right now?'

'Cool!' Aiden's grin almost split his thin, freckled face. 'Can I ring Mum to come and get me?'

Jack grinned. 'She's on her way.'

'Cool!' The youngster bounded up off the lounge. 'I'll get my stuff—'

'Hey!' Jack called him back. 'What about thanking Sister Wilde? She's looked after you pretty well, hasn't she?'

'Yeah...' Aiden looked sheepish. 'Thanks, Sister.'

'You're welcome, Aiden.' Geena placed a hand on his shoulder. 'Want a hand to organise your gear?'

He shook his head. 'Piers'll help me. He's cool.'

'Piers is really good with him.' Geena was still smiling as they walked back up the ward.

'It's not easy when kids are world-weary at twelve years old.' Jack's bleeper went. He looked at it for a second and then pocketed it. 'Are we still on for tonight?'

His blue eyes searched her face and Geena blinked uncertainly. Did he want an out? Was he regretting his invitation already? But, then, it wasn't like a date or anything, she rationalised swiftly. More like colleagues showing the flag...

She gave a strained little laugh. 'Cassie is beating the jungle drums already. It'd probably cause more talk if we didn't turn up than if we do...'

'Let's give 'em their money's worth, then.' He flashed her a grin. 'I'm picking you up about nine, aren't I?'

Her heart jolted under her ribs and she licked her lips. 'Do you have my address?'

'I do.' Jack's gaze continued to roam over her

face. 'I gave you a lift home during that thunderstorm just before Christmas, remember?'

Geena bit her lip. She did—vaguely. But the ride had hardly been memorable. And he'd stopped for only seconds to let her out. 'I have the garden flat at the back,' she said a bit primly. 'There's a path at the side...' She wound to a halt, embarrassed. He was regarding her with heavy-lidded amusement.

'I'm a big boy, Geena,' he said softly. 'I'll find you.'

CHAPTER FOUR

THE two letters in Geena's mailbox brought a soft smile to her lips. She recognised her mother's handwriting and the typed envelope was from her sister, Anne-Maree. They were fat, too, which meant a nice long read.

Holding the letters against her chest, she unlocked the door of her flat and went inside, once again appreciating the convenience of her home. It was reasonably modern and close enough to the hospital for her to be able to walk to work.

Of course she still had her car. Her move from Sydney meant there were now lots of wonderful country places to explore and she'd already accomplished a fair bit of sightseeing on her days off.

Kicking off her shoes, she went to the fridge for a cool drink. A wry little smile touched her mouth. There was always Jack's farm when she ran out of places to explore. Perhaps he'd invite her there one day. Perhaps…

Strange how you could be wrong about people, she thought, making herself comfortable in the deep leather armchair. When she'd thought about the senior registrar in any personal sense, she'd placed him in some kind of streamlined bachelor apartment.

A muted tut left her mouth. She had to stop thinking about him. With a little sigh she closed her eyes and knew she couldn't. No matter how she tried to diffuse it, the warmth of his kiss was still there in her heart, her mind, on her lips.

The sheer knee-weakening lushness of it had stirred up emotions she'd almost forgotten. Perhaps not forgotten exactly but put on hold while she'd gone on playing the role of oldest sister.

With their mother at work, it had seemed natural for Anne-Maree and Vanessa to turn to Geena for support. And she'd certainly given plenty of that. Just last year she'd helped them organise their weddings, and had been a bridesmaid for each of them.

'Your turn next, Geena,' one of the guests had said laughingly when Geena had stuck out a hand to save herself from being jostled and had inadvertently caught Anne-Maree's bouquet.

She pulled a face and, taking a deep breath, made herself concentrate on her mother's long letter.

Geena drizzled water over the last potplant on her enclosed front porch and placed the watering-can back on its shelf. The long summer evening was drawing in, the vibrant pinks and yellows of the setting sun fading and disappearing over the horizon. It was cooler, the atmosphere lighter, as the world around deepened to dusk.

Geena realised she'd left herself barely enough time to get ready for the dance. Well, that's how she'd planned it, wasn't it? Anticipation, like fairy footsteps, tiptoed up her backbone as she turned and went back inside.

She showered, using her favourite gel, breathing in its subtle flowery perfume as she smoothed it over her skin.

Her hair received a swift shampoo and conditioning and seconds later she was wrapping herself in a huge fluffy towel.

With a hand that was slightly unsteady she flicked through the items in her bureau drawer. It seemed an occasion for her silkiest underwear. Not that anyone was going to see it. She laughed dryly at the crazy notion.

Thank heavens her hair was the least of her worries, she thought, picking up her hair-dryer and round-bristled brush. The cut was superb, letting the layers fall back just where they were supposed to.

Holding the dryer deftly, Geena ran her fingers through the longish strands on top, coaxing a few tendrils fashionably across her forehead.

Now for her dress. Sliding back the door of the wardrobe, she peered inside. There was only one choice she cared to make.

She spread the ruby-red silk concoction she'd

worn at Anne-Maree's wedding across the bed. With her head tipped on one side, she tapped a finger on her chin. A faintly speculative gleam lit her eyes.

Jack had said they should give their contemporaries their money's worth. Well, she could do that.

Geena was ready a few minutes before nine. Well, as ready as she'd ever be. Gnawing at her bottom lip thoughtfully, she smoothed a hand over her hip and wondered if she was showing too much of everything.

She had to admit the dress looked every bit as flattering as it had at Anne-Maree's wedding. The cut was straight and slim-fitting, the length fashionably almost to her ankles and the style was deceptively simple, the rich delustred fabric making its own statement. Shoestring straps held up the bodice, leaving her shoulders bare. A side-on twist in the mirror revealed the slit to her thigh.

With fingers that were suddenly like thumbs, she fastened a fine gold chain around her neck.

The doorbell pealed.

'Jack...' Geena blinked out into the soft light of the porch. At the sight of his rangy figure dressed casually in black trousers and black shirt with faint silver tracery, her pulse jumped then raced headlong to a mad beat, as if in silent recognition of this invisible pull of the senses that had been happening between them for most of the day.

She swallowed. 'Come in. I'm ready.'

'That you are.' Jack's eyes narrowed appreciatively as he stepped over the threshold and into the lounge. He whistled softly. 'That's some dress!'

'Oh!' Geena's hand flew to her throat. 'It's not too…? Well, I wasn't sure…'

His eyebrows lifted in wry admiration. 'Lady, you look fabulous.'

Colour winged along Geena's cheekbones. 'It's just a dress, Jack,' she remonstrated weakly, bending to activate the switch on the table lamp. Suddenly, she wished she'd opted for her black evening skirt and demure silk blouse.

Watching the play of emotions across her face, Jack tamped down the urge to haul her up against him and kiss her until they were both senseless. Instead, he shoved his hands in his pockets, pulling back from insanity just in time.

'Should we go?' Geena straightened, her stomach lurching at the directness of his gaze.

'Sure.' Jack's mouth compressed slightly. He scraped an impatient hand across his jaw. 'After you.'

'Thanks.' Sensation brushed the surface of her skin as he held open the door for her and followed her out.

His car, a low-slung moody-blue Celica, was

parked at the kerb. The dance was being held at the community centre adjoining the hospital grounds. Geena was glad. Glad they'd be there in a few minutes, leaving little time to make conversation in the car.

She teased at the inside of her cheek as she fastened her seat belt. He'd gone suddenly quiet. She wished she knew why. Oh, well, they needn't stay long at the valentine dance. Then he could bring her home and go back to his farm. Disappear up a hollow log for all she cared.

'Animals fed and watered?' Geena knew the question sounded stilted but someone had to say something.

'Ah, yes.' He manoeuvred the car swiftly out of her street. 'I haven't many at the moment, actually. A wallaby recovering from a dog attack and a couple of hairy-nosed wombats that were pouchers.'

'Pouchers?' Geena cast him a dry look. 'I'm a city girl, Jack, remember?'

'Oh, sorry. They were found in the pouch when their respective mothers were killed by road traffic. As a result the joeys have to be hand-reared.'

'Is that difficult?' Geena's tender heart was touched.

'Very. And I don't have the time to do any of that. These chaps I have now are getting on for a year old. I'll probably have them another few months before they're ready to be released in the wild to set up their own burrow. Looking forward to the dance?' He changed the conversation abruptly as he turned into the hospital car park, making for his allotted space.

'Of course,' Geena said too brightly.

Oh, heavens. Was this a huge mistake? Geena gave a hurried look around her as Jack helped her from the car.

'By the sound of it, things are rocking,' he said.

Her head came up and she listened. 'They must have hired a disc jockey.' A poignant love song throbbed out into the night air. Under the overhead lights she looked at Jack and winced. 'Surely they're not going to play that stuff all night?'

Jack's mouth gave an expressive twist. 'I believe someone told me it's Valentine's Day.' With clever footwork he dodged Geena's swipe, retaliating by capturing her hand and drawing her to his side.

Geena took an uncomfortable swallow, feeling his fingers flex between hers. Tighten. The soft fabric of his trousers brushed against her bare thigh. 'Jack…'

'What?' He skated a thumb pad over her knuckles. 'Don't you like me touching you?'

Of course she did. Too darned much…

'Hey, you two! Wait a minute!' Mary Duffy and her husband, Derek Chalmers, were making their way in from the street. 'Isn't this great fun?' Mary said in her soft Irish lilt as they drew level.

'Poor baby.' Derek looped an arm around his wife's shoulders, hugging her. 'Indulge her. She doesn't get out much.' The remark earned him a dig from Mary's elbow. 'Ouch!' Derek gave a mock yelp and pretended his ribs were fractured.

Jack shook his head at Geena. 'And there we were imagining this was a party for the grown-ups!'

Geena's apprehension began to fade. With a sense of unreality she allowed herself to be swept along with the crowd, joining in the banter when she could, hugging Jack's side when she couldn't.

And Krista had panicked that no one would turn up! Geena couldn't believe the crowd that packed the big hall. She must remember to congratulate Krista and the rest of the committee on a job well done.

As Cassie had promised, there were places for her and Jack at the A and E department's table. A little overwhelmed, Geena took in the scene, smiling at the sea of faces. Fluttering a wave here and there. There seemed so much glamour—among the women at least—and Geena was very glad she'd worn the red dress.

'Very exotic!' Cassie voiced the low, throaty comment in Geena's ear before her fiancé, Brad, whisked the senior nurse onto the dance floor.

'Told you so,' Jack murmured in her other ear. 'Fancy a drink?'

Geena coloured faintly and placed her squashy

little evening bag on the table in front of her. 'A wine spritzer might be nice.'

'Mary?' Jack asked. 'Same for you?'

'Oh, lovely. Thanks, Jack.'

'I'll come with you,' Derek said, and the two men wandered companionably across to the bar.

'Are you and Jack—you know?' Mary rocked her hand expressively, an indulgent smile tickling her lips.

Geena bit her lip. She liked Mary, trusted her and her down-to-earth way of assessing things, but she hardly knew herself what—if anything—was happening between her and Jack O'Neal. 'We're here tonight to represent the children's ward, Mary. And we're friends, of course,' she added lamely. 'Good friends.'

'Oh, yes,' the SR responded in a singsong voice. 'And I'm Father Christmas. In Casualty we're trained to be observant. I'd say our Jacko fancies you like mad.'

Geena felt the slow beat of colour on her cheeks and opened her mouth to deny it, but then the men appeared with the drinks and there were toasts all round, silly jokes, more banter.

'You OK?' Jack trailed his fingertips over the bare skin of Geena's back where his arm was draped along the top of her chair.

'Fine,' she lied, leaning forward and disengaging his hand.

'Oh, Lord,' he groaned. 'I think I'll slide under the table. Here comes Krista!'

'Stop it!' Geena choked on a laugh. The junior RN was indeed making straight for their table, her mission clearly evident.

'Raffle tickets, anyone?' Her blonde head held high, Krista flapped the books of tickets, dimpling at the males around the table.

'I'm out, Kris.' Jack held up his hands in self-defence. 'I've bought enough tickets to paper the loo.'

'OK.' Krista gave a soft laugh. 'You're excused. Dr Chalmers?'

'What's the prize? And it's Derek.'

'Oh, right.' Krista swooped a coy look from under her long lashes. 'It's a week for two on the Gold Coast plus flights to and from.'

Derek gave a low whistle and dug out his wallet. 'I'd kill for that.'

'I'd better alert your patients,' Mary quipped drily, draping a hand across his shoulder.

Geena saw a note of the highest denomination pass hands and blinked.

'Did you want change, Dr— Derek?' Krista was busily separating the tickets from their butts.

Derek's eyebrow peaked. 'How many chances will that give me?'

'A hundred.'

He nodded. 'That'll do it.'

'Good grief!' Jack shook his head in amazement when Krista left their table and moved to her next quarry. 'That girl should be a bookmaker.'

Derek looked blank. 'I thought she was.'

'Idiot!' Mary ruffled the back of her husband's neatly combed head. 'Come and dance with me.'

'What about you?' Jack turned to Geena. 'Would you like to dance?'

Geena glanced up quickly, her eyes colliding with the fathomless blue of his gaze. She made a faint moue. 'I suppose we could shuffle around.'

Lifting a hand, he slowly tucked a tendril of dark hair behind her ear. 'I wouldn't have taken you for a shuffler, Geena. More of a...glider, I think.'

She drew back, hearing her stilted laugh. The silly conversation was doing crazy things to her insides, fuelling the curl in the pit of her stomach. She propped her chin on her upturned hand. 'How would you rate yourself?' she asked blandly.

'Hmm.' His eyes had a musing gleam. 'A good all-rounder perhaps? I got a prize for disco dancing when I was a teenager.' He pretended to puff out his chest.

Geena sent her gaze heavenward and then looked startled as he shot back his chair and pulled them both upright. 'We're not about to attempt that, are we?' she squeaked.

Jack snorted. 'We're in big trouble if we are. They're playing ''Moon River''. Come on.'

Geena found herself in his arms. Well and truly. And it was so easy, she thought. So easy to let go, to let herself sway to the rhythm, to go where Jack wanted to take her.

She closed her eyes as he tucked her head against his shoulder. Was this the missing element? she wondered, burrowing in against him. The *something* she'd wanted all her life without even knowing it existed?

When the music stopped she felt as if she'd come out of a dream.

'Geena?'

She raised her head and looked at him, frowning slightly as if she were seeing him for the first time. Something was happening between them—if it hadn't already. Acknowledging it, though, that might be a different matter entirely.

Taking a deep breath, she sought desperately for lightness. 'You're not a bad dancer, Dr O'Neal. Scrub up well, too.' She tapped her fingertips against the lapel of his collar. 'Nice shirt.'

His smile was crooked and his hand came up and covered hers. 'Belinda got it for me on her last trip to Rome.'

Geena raised an eyebrow. 'Your sister has wonderful taste. Does she like her job as a flight attendant?'

He laughed shortly. 'Oh, no, you don't, Sister Wilde.' Taking her hand firmly, he began to lead her off the dance floor. 'We're going to get some supper and you get to tell me all about *your* family.'

'Now, I'm off to get us coffee.' Gathering up their plates Jack got decisively to his feet. 'Don't go away.'

As if she would. Geena looked about her. They'd taken their food out onto the verandah and had managed to secure a reasonably secluded table by a large arrangement of golden palm fronds.

She wondered briefly about the others at their table but they'd seemed to be doing their own thing, as she and Jack were…

'You were quick.' She looked up as Jack arrived back at their table, her eyes widening. 'You've got dessert as well.'

'Brenda's contribution, apparently. I couldn't say no.' His grin was infectious and he plonked the loaded plate in front of her.

'What is it?'

'Plum and polenta slice.' Jack passed her a serviette. 'Looked too good to pass up.'

Geena made a small sound in her throat. 'After the lunch I ate, I'm amazed I could find room for anything. But this does look delicious,' she admitted ruefully, forking up a section of the crumbly pastry.

'Tell me about your family.'

They were halfway through their coffee when Jack made the soft request.

Geena picked up her cup, gaining time. So far the evening had surrounded her with a drugged kind of unreality and Jack's request had sparked thoughts she would rather have left for another time.

'I'm the oldest of three sisters,' she said evenly. 'Anne-Maree works in a path lab and Vanessa teaches high school. My mother manages a dress shop.'

'And your father?'

Geena blinked. 'He left when I was eight.'

'That must have been tough.'

She surveyed him with unblinking eyes. 'We survived.'

Jack's long fingers toyed with the spoon in his saucer. 'Nevertheless, it must have been difficult.'

Geena's eyelids dropped, shielding her expression. The last thing she needed was for him to start feeling sorry for her. 'Of course it was difficult.' She took a quick gulp of coffee. 'Especially for my mother. It taught me one thing at least,' she added, her control slipping just a fraction. 'I'll never allow myself to go down that road.'

His snort bordered on harshness. 'How do you intend to ensure that, Geena? There are no guarantees in any marriage.'

A frown touched her forehead. 'You sound like you know, Jack.'

He shrugged. 'I don't know anything.'

'Well, I still think my father fell far short of giving it his best shot,' she persisted.

He was silent for a moment, while the summer-warm breeze wafted along the verandah, whispering through the palms, rattling their stiff foliage. 'Except that for some people even their best shot is not enough. Have you considered that, Geena?'

Further conjecture was stifled by the arrival of Derek and Mary. 'So, this is where you got to!' Mary leaned back against her husband and his arms came round to link across her midriff. 'We were going to invite you to share a coffee with us but you've obviously almost finished.'

'Anxious to get back on the dance floor, are you?' Derek joked.

Geena's gaze misted. She glanced quickly at her watch. 'Actually, I wouldn't mind leaving now, Jack. I've plans for tomorrow.' She hadn't, but it wouldn't hurt to let him think she had.

One look at her face and Jack got swiftly to his feet. He moved to hold back her chair but she was there before him.

His mouth drew in. He'd upset her, pressing her about her family. And he didn't know why he had. Unless it was to try to rationalise his own feelings of guilt, inadequacy or whatever the hell they were.

Their farewells to the other couple were brief.

'Don't do anything we wouldn't do,' Derek called jokingly after them.

Geena cringed inwardly at the tired old cliché. She stifled a sigh. The evening had begun with such promise. Now she and Jack seemed poles apart. She'd struck him on a nerve somewhere, disturbed some kind of emotional baggage. Emotion clouded her eyes. 'I didn't mean to drag you away early, Jack.'

'You didn't.' His touch on her arm was fleeting yet it prickled with electricity, re-igniting the awareness between them, sending its message flaring through her veins. 'Hang on,' he said when they got to his car. 'I'll unlock the door for you.'

Once they were settled and belted in, he said, 'As a fund-raiser, I'd say it was a very successful evening, wouldn't you?' He started the engine, reversed the car in a semicircle and shot towards the exit.

Geena swallowed, feeling the tension knotting inside her. 'Yes, it was,' she agreed flatly.

They arrived back at her flat far too quickly. Out of the corner of her eye Geena was aware of Jack cutting the engine. Moving quickly, she fumbled for the release catch on her seat belt. 'Thanks for your company this evening, Jack.'

'Don't go for a minute.' He scraped a hand through his hair and then, leaning forward, propped his arm on the steering-wheel. The brush of his shirtsleeve on her bare skin sent Geena's composure out of the window. 'I want to apologise,' he said huskily.

'For what?'

He grimaced. 'My holier-than-thou comments earlier.'

Her head lowered. Geena ran her thumb across the raised pattern on her evening bag. 'You caught me off guard. I—didn't mean to sound bitter.'

'You didn't.' He was quick to refute her. 'And if you did, God knows, you probably have reason to be.'

She shrugged, an almost unnoticeable lift of one shoulder. 'I always felt loved, Jack. My mother saw to that. And if I didn't have both parents for most of the time, well, so what? Lots of people don't.'

'No.' Automatically, he lifted a hand and shrugged his seat belt away. 'But I think now I understand your natural empathy with the sole-parent families on the ward.'

Geena made a small face. 'Don't beat yourself up, Jack. You're not short on perception yourself.'

'I was this morning.' His mouth turned down. 'With the Lynch case.' He leaned marginally closer to stare at her, his eyes very soft in the moonlight.

Geena blinked, meeting his gaze with difficulty. All kinds of emotions began threading their way through her mind. But he was right. His response had been out of character, almost harsh. Logically, something about Claudia Lynch and her son's accident must have triggered it. She swallowed the dryness in her throat. 'Want to tell me about it?'

His outburst of laughter was raw around the edges. 'Got a year or two?'

Without ceremony he helped her out of the car and walked her to her door. They stood closely together, the porch light elongating their shadows against the wall. Should she ask him in? Geena didn't know. Just the thought of it tripped her pulse and made her heart beat faster.

'Got your key?' he asked softly, and Geena pressed the metal object into his outstretched hand.

Jack unlocked the door and let it stand open. The lounge room with its softly lit ambience seemed to draw their eyes.

'Are you coming in?' Geena's voice sounded thick and vaguely husky.

'Perhaps not.' Lifting a hand, he cupped her cheek, brushing his thumb along the length of her jaw. 'Still friends?' he asked gruffly.

'Why wouldn't we be?' Geena's heart was thudding. Turning quickly, she fled through the door. 'Goodnight, Jack,' she said, before closing it with a click, leaning against it and squeezing her eyes shut.

What a disaster! Whatever they might have hoped for was finished before they'd even begun to take the first few steps. Now the chemistry was muddied, leaving them unable to go forward, yet too much had happened to allow them to go back...

Which left them where? she wondered bleakly as she creamed off her make-up, brushed her teeth and climbed into bed.

Next morning Geena woke early to the strident hum of the lawnmower. With a muttered expletive, she buried her head under the pillow, wanting to strangle the perpetrator.

A few minutes later, she gave up the fight for any chance of a lie-in. Instead, she threw herself out of bed and under the shower.

The pinpoints of warmth to every part of her body lulled her senses, letting her thoughts roam free. Oh, Lord. Geena's fingers tightened on her upper arms. She'd acted like a complete ninny when Jack had brought her home.

She felt herself cringe inwardly. Why on earth hadn't she handled things like a reasonably sensible adult, instead of bolting inside like a startled rabbit?

Her hollow laughter bounced off the tiled walls. Even a rabbit would have had more sense!

CHAPTER FIVE

JACK took his coffee outside to the back patio. Misty, his mother's large grey cat, was occupying the squatter's chair.

'Find your own turf, mate,' he said moodily, unceremoniously hoisting the animal out of its berth, only to receive Misty's baleful green stare as he stalked off, tail whipping resentfully.

'It's a tough old world,' Jack muttered, collapsing back into the depths of the soft canvas and stretching his jeans-clad legs along the extended wooden arms of the outdoor chair.

He clasped his coffee to his chest.

'Geena.' Just saying her name aloud afforded the luxury of release.

Taking a mouthful of coffee, he grimaced. He'd acted like an inept fool last night. In the clear light of day he couldn't believe it! Was he so hopelessly out of touch? He must be.

He looked down into the black brew. He should have gone inside when she'd invited him, let the evening wind down naturally, instead of ending it so awkwardly on her front porch. Good grief! Would it have been so difficult?

Surely they could have listened to some music,

talked. Talked, heck! He closed his eyes and felt his heart pounding. In his mind he kissed her...her eyes, her temple, her mouth...

He made a sound of disgust in the back of his throat and jackknifed upright. Frustration was eating him alive. He hadn't felt this kind of urgency since, well, since Zoe...

Swallowing the rest of his coffee, he pulled himself out of the chair. He had to move on with his life. Common sense told him it was crazy, perhaps even pathetic, to have allowed Zoe to remain the focus of his baffled anger for so long. Three years was far too long to dwell on what might have been.

Shaking his head as if to clear it, he wandered across to the railings where his eyes travelled out over the summer landscape, the rust-like texture of the rolling plains and beyond to the grey-green bushland lapping the feet of the sandstone cliff at the edge of his property.

He stared down into the soft, leafy shade plants of the rockery. God, it was like living with a permanent hangover. He should be able to forgive and forget. He had forgiven Zoe. He just couldn't forget...

Geena arrived at work promptly on Monday morning. She had no idea how to approach Jack but one of them would have to say something. Her heart dipped. His car was already in its space.

She made her way to the staffroom, half expecting to find him there, but he was nowhere to be seen. Instead, her own team for the early shift was there, along with a few stragglers who were coming off night duty.

'Oh, Geena,' a bright-eyed Krista said eagerly. 'We made heaps from the dance.'

'Your committee did a marvellous job, Kris.' Geena smiled. 'Congratulations!'

'Oh, thanks.' The junior sister gave a self-deprecating little shrug. 'We introduced a few new things. That helped. And the raffle, of course.'

'Who won it?' someone asked. 'We left before it was drawn.'

'Brad Lomax.' Krista surveyed the expectant faces. 'Cassie Gordon's fiancé. Isn't it great?'

'I expect they'll use it as a honeymoon trip,' Brenda said. Opening her locker, she bundled her bag inside. 'Dr Chalmers would have been disappointed. I believe he spent a small fortune on tickets.'

'He did OK.' Krista waved a hand airily. 'He won the consolation prize, a case of fine wine.'

'Do we all get a say in how the money is used on behalf of the kids?' Megan looked hopefully around the group.

'There's such a lot we could do,' Krista bubbled excitedly. 'My cousin works at Oakleigh Children's in Sydney,' she went on. 'They've just had this new play area put in. It's designed on the theme of the beach. Even got wave-shaped ceilings.' She waggled her hand in illustration.

Geena bit back a wry smile. She doubted whether Hopeton could run to that. Still, it was heartening to see such interest from the younger members of staff.

'Perhaps everyone could get their ideas together by the end of the week,' she said. 'We'll have an informal meeting, decide what's practical and present our suggestions to management. OK?'

With the report taken and duties allocated, Geena paused for breath. There were a dozen things waiting for her attention but suddenly she decided they could wait. She had to talk to Jack or she'd be useless for the rest of the shift. Before she could change her mind, she walked along the corridor and knocked on his door.

'Yes?' Jack was on the phone and, after glancing up briefly, he waved her to a chair.

Heart thrumming, Geena sat, her hands pressed tightly on her knees. After a second she stole a look at him. His rumpled theatre scrubs and shadowed jaw told their own story. He looked utterly weary. She swallowed, watching as he wound up his call and clipped the receiver back on its rest.

'Did you want me for something?' He leaned back in his chair, his look faintly guarded.

Geena shook her head. 'Just touching base,' she

said with a taut little smile. 'You look tired. Were you called in?'

'Long old night.' He shrugged philosophically. 'I assisted Ellis Greer in surgery. Orthopaedic job on a lad of eleven, Daniel DeVere.'

'RTA?' Geena frowned, imagining the chaos.

'Not this time.' Jack spun his arms to half-mast and stretched. 'Trail-bike accident. Daniel took the cattle grid at speed and lost control. Wrapped himself around the steel guard rails.'

Geena winced. 'Kids can be so foolhardy, can't they? Big damage?'

Jack nodded. 'And a lengthy rehab. We had to pin and plate both his legs. Tib and fib on both sides completely smashed. Left arm iffy. Still in ICU, of course.'

'When can we expect him down?' Geena asked. The child would need careful orientation before he came into the ward for such a long stay.

'Barring complications...' Jack considered his fingertips for a moment. 'Tomorrow afternoon, I'd say. I'll leave it to you to visit the ICU when you can manage it. Do the usual.' His grin was weary and a bit lopsided.

She nodded. 'I should get a chance around lunchtime. Parents still with him?'

'Mum is, I think. Dad had to get back. Said he had sheep to crutch.'

'Ugh!' Geena made a face. 'That sounds disgusting!'

'It is, believe me.' The quirk at the corners of Jack's mouth extended to a chuckle as he swung out of his chair. 'I'm glad to see you, Geena,' he said softly, parking himself on the corner of the desk next to her.

Geena took a quick breath. 'What time did you finish up in Theatre?'

'Fivish.'

'Why on earth didn't you go home?' She blinked in astonishment. 'Or at least get a bed here for a few hours?'

His eyes turned hazy. 'I decided to have a shower and wait for you...' He studied her for a moment and then, raising his hand, he began slowly to run his fingertips along the outer edge of her ear. 'I had a miserable weekend.'

Geena felt herself shaking from the outside in. His touch was like an electric current, so exquisite it was almost painful, penetrating every part of her body. She felt stunned, unable to move or think. But she had to think, to say what she'd come to say...

'Jack...about Friday night,' she said breathlessly. 'I acted like a ninny. I practically slammed the door in your face—'

'I probably deserved it.' He seemed totally in

control, shifting his hand to her nape and letting it rest there. 'I wanted to come in, Geena.'

'Did you?' With a sharp movement, she set her elbow on the desk and turned her face towards him. 'But you seemed so...'

'Switched off?' His mouth worked for a minute. 'Out of practice, more like. I'm still a bit gun-shy, I suppose.' His laugh was hollow. 'Swimming in the shallows.'

'Why...?' The query seemed to linger on the air.

'Divorce is never a great confidence-builder.'

'Oh, Jack...' Like quicksilver, Geena spun upright, moving straight into his arms, as he straightened and gathered her in.

Geena didn't say a word. Couldn't. She was only conscious of the thud of his heart through the thin cotton of his scrub top.

'I can't believe any of this.' Jack drew back and looked deeply into her eyes. 'You and me,' he said huskily. 'Geena...' Taking her face between his hands, he tipped her head back gently.

Geena closed her eyes, her breath erupting in a little sigh as he took her mouth and she felt her safe world explode.

His kiss sought everything from her. His tongue coaxed until she complied in a ritual as old as time. A love dance.

Jack... She said his name in her head and her fingers dug into the cord of his shoulders. His mouth left hers only to return to savour her sweetness again and again.

When he finally lifted his head Geena kept her eyes closed, holding on to him for the few seconds it took to regain reality.

'Open your eyes,' he said throatily. She did and they stared at each other. Jack captured her hand, closed it and raised it to his lips. He shook his head in wonderment. 'This is real, isn't it?'

Dear God, she hoped so. Geena felt breathless, as if she'd been tossed high on a huge wave and carried, half drowning, to the shore. 'Jack...' She slid her fingers down his arm, halting when they encountered his wristwatch. Reality stepped in. 'I should get back...'

'Should you...?' His head bent towards her, his mouth teasingly urgent against her top lip, the corner of her mouth. 'When are you coming home with me?'

Geena's breath jammed in her throat. It's happened, she thought, and it's like a dream—one she wanted never to end. She wanted Jack O'Neal, needed him like her own breath. Her eyes locked with his, fascinated by the startling blueness in their depths. 'Next weekend?'

He groaned. 'That's for ever!' He laughed softly, protest still in his voice. 'But I suppose I'll survive.' He hugged her back into his arms and then reluctantly let her go.

Geena went to the door and turned. Their eyes met again, as if they were both reluctant to let go of the magic surrounding them.

Jack's laugh was low and a bit rusty. 'I feel as if I could run a marathon,' he said.

And well he might, Geena thought with a little lurch in her stomach. With his rumpled hair, his eyes ablaze, his goofy grin, he looked so wonderfully *alive*.

Her teeth caught on her bottom lip as she smiled. 'Get some sleep, Jack.'

Pressed against the wall next to his office a few moments later, Geena tried to still the clamour inside her. She craved some quiet time and mental space but she knew that at that moment she had the luxury of neither.

Taking a shaking breath, she pressed her hands against her cheeks for a moment before she made her way back to the station.

Her step faltered. Jack's resident, Toni Michaels, was hovering, obviously waiting to do rounds.

'Morning, Toni.' Geena reined in her bemusement with a taut smile. 'Won't be a tick.'

'No hurry,' the resident said evenly, leaning her elbows on the counter. 'Good weekend?'

'So-so.' Geena began collecting files from their pigeon-holes. 'It was too hot to get energetic. Except for the valentine dance,' she qualified drily. 'Were you there?'

'No.' Toni went a pretty shade of pink. 'I had a dinner date with Phil Carter.'

Geena blinked, startled. She hoped Toni knew what she was doing. In the month he'd been relieving, the quietly spoken, fair-haired Canadian doctor had made quite an impact on the female staff at Hopeton, though as far as Geena knew the man was married. He'd even shown her pictures of his children, for heaven's sake!

'Phil and his wife are legally separated.' Toni seemed anxious to set the record straight. 'He had his two little girls up for the weekend. They're so cute, Geena.' Toni's green eyes lit up. 'We had a great time together.'

'I'm glad for you, Toni,' Geena said, and meant it.

It was only when they were halfway through the ward round that her conversation with Toni struck a warning chord in Geena's brain and refused to be dislodged.

The thought that Jack might have a child—or children—was oddly disturbing.

'Who's next?' Toni tucked a red-gold strand of hair behind her ear.

'Sophie Brennan's back with us, I'm afraid.' With an effort Geena dragged her thoughts back to practicalities. She handed the chart for the thirteen-year-old asthmatic to the resident. 'Jack admitted her last night.'

'Poor kid.' Toni pursed her lips thoughtfully. 'What's the betting her father's still smoking around her?'

'Perhaps not.' Jack materialised beside them. 'I'll take over now, Toni,' he said smoothly. 'Why don't you go to breakfast?'

'Oh, thanks, Jack.' With a wry smile she handed him the notes. 'I did make a rather early start.'

'And I'm grateful.' Lifting his hand, he shooed the young doctor off and then bent his dark head to Geena. 'You OK?'

Still reeling from their earlier encounter, Geena clung to the edge of the trolley. 'I thought you were going to get some sleep?'

'That can wait. Suddenly I feel full of energy.' One dark brow lifted. 'I wonder why?'

Geena took in a breath, her eyes running over him. He'd shaved and was very casually dressed in khaki trousers, a short-sleeved dark green shirt and desert boots. Which was probably what he'd thrown on when he'd been called in last night, she decided, flushing slightly. 'I'll...um...pass on that, if you don't mind.' She moved the trolley forward. 'Did you want to check on Sophie now?'

'Let's.'

Sophie was perched high against the pillows, her eyes following the antics of a cartoon character on the small television screen. Turning away from the television, she gave the health professionals a resigned look as they approached the bed.

'Let's see how you're doing, Sophie.' His expression intent, Jack ran his stethoscope over the girl's chest and back.

'I'm feeling better.' She turned huge violet eyes hopefully on the registrar. 'Can I go home?'

'Sorry, sweetheart.' Jack placed his hand gently against her dark head. 'No can do. Not until we have you stable again.'

She sighed. 'Daddy's not smoking any more.'

'I know and that's good.' Jack parked himself on the edge of the bed. 'So, we'll have to see what the fuss is about this time, won't we?'

'I s'pose.' Sophie shrugged her thin shoulders. 'I hate all this stuff I have to do!' Her mouth wobbled.

'Like what?' Jack leaned forward, listening.

'Like having the drip, the nebuliser, the Ventolin. And everyone telling me to drink lots of water, cough up...' She drew to a halt, tears welling suddenly in her eyes.

'Honey, we know it's hard.' Geena stepped in swiftly, straightening the pillows and smoothing the blue counterpane across Sophie's slender frame. She cupped her hand around the teenager's cheek. 'We're not that mean and nasty, are we?'

'N-no.' Sophie gave a muffled giggle and brushed the backs of her hands against her eyes.

'Ah, that sounds like lunch.' Jack looked at his watch and frowned. 'Or is it dinner?'

'It's morning tea, silly!' Sophie cast him an exasperated look.

'So it is.' Jack caught Geena's eye and smothered a grin. 'Got something to read, Sophie?'

She nodded. 'Mum's bringing some library books in later. And my knitting.'

'You can knit?' He looked astounded.

Sophie fingered the end of her plait. 'I'm knitting a scarf in my football team's colours,' she said importantly.

Jack got to his feet, his stethoscope dangling from his fingers. 'And what team might that be?'

The youngster sent her eyes heavenwards. 'Hopeton Warriors, of course!'

'Of course,' Jack echoed, his face very straight.

Geena sensed his preoccupation as they made their way back to the nurses' station. 'Is Sophie in for a long stay this time?'

'Don't know yet.' Jack shook his head. 'For starters I'll put her down for some physio. Ask Mark to increase the percussion on her back, would you? We've got to get that cough productive somehow. And another thing, Geena.' He took out his pen and began writing quickly. 'Have a chat to Sophie about whether she's done anything different in the last day or so.'.

'Whether she's had a change of environment perhaps?'

'Environment, food, whatever. Her asthma's fairly well managed now and her mother watches Sophie's diet.'

'She doesn't buy food at the school tuckshop any longer either,' Geena confirmed. 'On account of the minefield pertaining to additives.'

'Mmm.' Jack tugged thoughtfully at his bottom lip. 'Just run through what she's been up to. It may turn up something. Now I'm off home to check on my animals.' His mouth folded in a smile and he handed Sophie's file back to her. 'Back soon. Phil's around if you need back-up.'

Geena watched him as he waited for the lift, the line of his shoulders under the soft cotton shirt, the long muscles of his back, his profile. She took an unsteady breath. Was she already in love with him?

CHAPTER SIX

IT WAS almost noon by the time Geena managed to get time to visit the ICU. She took Megan with her, giving the student details of Daniel's accident as they rode up in the lift.

'It won't be a pretty sight,' the charge warned. 'Our job is to prepare him—and his parents for that matter—for quite a long stay in hospital. Would you like to be involved in Daniel's care, Megan?'

The third-year nodded. 'If you think I can do it, Sister?'

'Of course you can do it,' Geena said bracingly. 'You'll be a first-rate nurse at the end of your training. I certainly haven't seen anything that would indicate the contrary.'

Megan flushed with pleasure. 'I'm really tuned in to the kids. At least, I think I am.'

'Well, if you decide to make paediatrics your speciality, you should try for a post-grad place in one of the big children's hospitals somewhere.'

'Is that what you did?' Megan asked pertly.

Geena raised an eyebrow amusedly. 'More or less. Right, here we are,' she said as the lift stopped at the IC floor.

IC sister, Adrienne Locke, beckoned them into

Daniel's room. 'His mum's just stepped out for a breather,' she said.

'Why don't you do the same?' Geena said quietly. 'We'll be here for a bit.'

'Well, if you don't mind.' The sister sent a wry look towards her young patient. 'Daniel is certainly not going anywhere in a hurry.'

That was only too evident. Geena's mouth firmed. What a mess for this poor kid.

He was surrounded by drips and drains, both legs elevated on orthopaedic pillows, external fixators applied to each of his legs.

'Hi, Daniel.' Geena bent over the boy. 'I'm Geena.' She touched a hand to his reddish-brown hair. 'In a day or so you'll be coming down to us to the children's ward, OK?'

Daniel's eyes flickered. 'Yuck. Do I have to?'

Geena exchanged a dry smile with Megan. The child was still groggy from the morphine drip but, nevertheless, it appeared they might be in for a long battle. Rehabilitation, especially for kids, was hardly ever easy.

Within a few minutes the ICU sister was back, followed by Mrs DeVere. Geena moved quickly.

'Could we have a word, please?' Geena forstalled the child's mother in the little anteroom. She introduced herself and then asked, 'How are you feeling?'

'Bewildered.' Marion DeVere shook her head.

'Danny's our only child...' She bit her lips together. 'I just wish I could take the pain for him...'

'Of course you do.' Geena's hand covered the mother's. 'But, rest assured, we'll try to keep Daniel as pain-free as possible.' Speaking quietly, Geena went on to explain the need for both his parents' co-operation in their son's rehabilitation.

'It won't always be easy, looking on,' Geena emphasised. 'And if you have any problem with anything to do with Daniel's care, come straight to me. All right?'

'Thank you, Sister.' The woman's gaze swung back towards her son's room. 'You've all been very kind. I never thought...' Tears welled in her eyes.

'Is your husband able to get in at all today?' Geena felt a pang of concern. In the mother's exhausted state, she was almost risking becoming a patient herself.

'He said he'd try for this afternoon.'

Geena nodded. 'Daniel is quite stable, Mrs DeVere. Perhaps you'd feel confident enough to leave him tonight? That way you could be back rested for his move to the children's ward tomorrow.'

'As soon as that?' Marion DeVere pushed a long strand of hair back over her shoulder.

'Oh, yes.' Geena got to her feet. 'We'll have your son feeling much more cheerful quite soon.'

The mother shook her head. 'But all those contraptions he's got on his legs...'

'I know.' Geena was sympathetic. 'It's all a bit daunting, isn't it? But we won't rush anything.'

'Bright kid.' Megan grinned as she and Geena rode back down in the lift. 'I had quite a chat to him while you were talking to his mum.'

'Handful?' Geena's full mouth tilted in a wry smile.

'I reckon!'

It was the next day at the nurses' station when Geena caught up properly with Jack. He'd had his clinic during the morning and Geena had been run off her feet in the ward.

'We've had another whooping-cough admission,' she told him, scanning a phone message from one of the children's parents. 'Jessica Mellis, aged seven. Phil did the necessary.'

'Damn!' he muttered. 'How many more?'

'Only time will tell.' Geena was realistic. 'Coffee?'

'Hmm? Oh, great, thanks. Join me?'

'Actually...' Geena glanced at her watch. 'I'm due for a break. I've brought sandwiches. Want to share?'

He looked at her oddly and Geena felt her face warm. Even as late as last week she'd not have dreamed of approaching Jack O'Neal this way. But surely things between them were different now? She swallowed. 'Jack?'

'Sorry, I was miles away. Um, that sounds good.' A sudden grin lit his face. 'Park?'

Geena sucked in her bottom lip. 'Dare we?'

He shrugged. 'May as well be hung for a sheep as a lamb, as my old grandad used to say. I'll grab us a couple of take-away coffees from the canteen. Meet you at the park entrance.'

'I've got fruit for afters.' Jack put the rosy apples next to the sandwiches and coffee.

'Lovely.' With fingers that shook slightly, Geena began setting out their impromptu picnic.

'This is a rare old treat, isn't it?' he murmured, sitting with his legs stretched out, his eyes half-closed against the sun.

'We were here last Friday,' she pointed out wryly, dividing the sandwiches neatly. Sliding his share onto a blue-and-white-checked paper napkin, she handed them across to him. 'It's cold beef and mustard,' she said. 'And there's some cress here if you want to spice them up a bit.'

'Terrific.' He cast her an amused little smile. 'Didn't plan all this, did you, Geena?'

She laughed, a soft gurgle in her throat, and coloured a bit. 'That's for me to know and you to find out, isn't it?'

His teeth glinted in a smile that did those odd things to her stomach. 'I accept the challenge.'

They were almost finished lunch when Geena turned her face to the sky and smiled. It was a beautiful day again, the midday sunlight bouncing off the crisp dark leaves of the eucalypts.

I could sit here for ever, she thought, lulled by the ceaseless whirring of the cicadas in the nearby shrubbery and entertained by the tiny busy finches as they flipped and flittered in and around the trellised jasmine and honeysuckle.

Little groups of personnel began to trickle across from the hospital, all obviously with the same idea of spending their precious off-duty time outdoors.

'Would you mind if we talked shop for a bit?' Resolutely, Geena brought her thoughts back to the present and began gathering up their lunch wrappings for the bin.

'Not if it means we can justify sitting here for a few more minutes.' Jack tossed an apple into the air and caught it.

Geena smiled. 'I guess we'll call it a case conference, then.' Against her better judgement she watched as his strong teeth cleaved a path through the crisp skin of the apple. The sheer physicality of it made her turn away quickly but nothing could have prevented the breathtaking ripple in her veins. She took a quick breath. 'I've had a chat to Sophie.'

'And?' Jack's dark brows winged upwards.

'She did have a change of environment. Last weekend. She went on a camp with her drama group. Apparently, they're whipping their first production for the year into shape. Our Sophie's the lead.'

Jack grinned. 'Good for her. Where did they go? Did she say?'

'Mmm...' Geena squeezed her eyes shut and then opened them with a snap. 'Taylor's Ridge.'

'I know it.' He swung upright, walking the few paces to deposit his apple core in the bin. 'They have cabins and so on. They're let out for school camps as well. Been there for ever.'

'So it could be the source of her episode.' Propping her chin on her upturned hand, Geena looked questioningly at him.

'Dust mites of some kind?' Jack anchored himself across the corner of the picnic table. 'Or bedding? Plus the additional stress of performing, even if she loves it.'

'And there was another thing.' Geena was thoughtful. 'Sophie was a bit shy about telling me, but she started her first period during last week.'

'Ah!' Jack nodded in satisfaction. 'Afflicted with hormones as well. Poor kid. More emotional upheaval. No wonder she ended up wheezing like an old fiddle on Sunday.'

'Apparently, her parents were very worried about

her when she got home. Wanted to bring her straight to the hospital.'

'Sophie held out as usual.' His comment was dry. 'How was she this morning?'

'Stable, relaxed. She had a really good night.'

Jack grinned. 'We can probably let her go home, then.'

'She worries me a bit.' Geena shook her head. 'She's such a skinny little thing, all eyes.'

'I'd rather call her fine-boned, Geena. Like you,' he added softly.

Panic clogged Geena's throat. Suddenly all thumbs, she jammed the lid on her lunch box. 'Sophie told me she swims a lot...'

'Yes.' He glanced down at her. 'What do you do for exercise, Geena?'

Was it a loaded question? Colour whipped along her cheekbones. She shrugged and decided to take it at face value. 'I go to the gym a bit. And I also swim. Unfortunately, there's no club in Hopeton that services my favourite sport.'

'Which is?' Jack slid off the table and stood to attention.

'Fencing.'

'Fencing?' His eyes held laughing disbelief. 'As in?' He made a few mock thrusts in the air.

Geena clicked her tongue. 'If you were duelling with me like that, Jack O'Neal, I'd have you maimed. Or dead.'

A laugh rippled out of his throat as his head went back.

'It's not funny,' she flared. 'Fencing is a fabulous discipline. And I'm good.' Her chin came up proudly. 'Damned good.'

'I'll bet you are.' His voice was smoky-soft, his eyes admiring. 'With your grace, your lightness. Yes.' His mouth pursed in conjecture. 'I'll just bet you are.'

Sophie was not in her room.

'Track her down, would you, Geena?' Jack was short. 'And get on to Ellis Greer. See if he can give us an ETA for Daniel. I'll need to allocate time to speak with the parents.' His bleeper went. Checking it, he frowned and began to move away. 'Thanks for lunch,' he flung back over his shoulder.

Geena sighed and watched him go. He was swamped again, preoccupied. She went in search of Sophie, wondering whether her heart could stand the strain until the weekend.

Sophie almost skipped back to her room. 'Am I going home?' she asked.

'That's up to Dr O'Neal.' Geena kept her face straight with difficulty. 'Perhaps you could cross your fingers, though.'

'You're looking pretty good, young woman,' Jack declared when he'd completed Sophie's lengthy examination.

'So?' She looked at him with wide-eyed expectancy.

'Yes.' Jack grinned. 'You can go home.'

'Oh, excellent!'

'Want to phone your mum?' Geena had been quietly slipping Sophie's bits and pieces into her overnight case.

'Mum's teaching this week.' The child said matter-of-factly. 'I'll go to my nan's.'

'So, we'll organise a taxi as usual?' Geena tucked Sophie's knitting into a corner of her case.

'Yes, please,' Sophie said with all the grace of a star about to depart her audience.

'You're still using your preventer twice daily, aren't you, Sophie?' Jack began scribbling up the last of the notes.

'Of course.' She sent her eyes heavenwards. 'I keep it beside my toothbrush like you told me. That way I don't forget.'

'Good girl.' Jack leaned over and touched the tip of her nose. 'So, barring emergencies, I'll see you at your next clinic appointment.'

'OK.' She wound her arms around her slender midriff. 'Thank you, Dr O'Neal, for looking after me.'

'Thank *you*, Sophie.' Jack dipped his head in a courteous little bow. 'You've been a model patient.' He moved to the door and then turned. 'Oh, by the way, knock 'em dead on opening night. Yes?'

Sophie flashed a grin that lit up her pixie-like little face like a neon sign. 'I will,' she promised.

When she'd waved goodbye to Sophie, Geena began taking Megan through the procedure for when Daniel would come on the ward. In normal circumstances she would have left it to Piers but her deputy was on days off. He'd been looking a bit stressed lately, she thought. Tasha's morning sickness was really taking its toll on their marriage.

'How long will the fixators have to stay in, Sister?'

'Oh, six to eight weeks most probably.' Geena gave a small grimace. 'Realise, Megan, it's going to be a heck of a job, keeping Daniel cheerful.'

'But also a challenge.' The student's small, neat hands came together in a little gesture of resolve.

'OK. We've got the orthopaedic bed ready.' Geena began to tick off her fingers. 'Two wardsmen to transfer him and Brenda and I will help with the lift and you'll hold the drip steady. Then, while we settle Daniel in, Dr O'Neal will be on hand to have a chat to the parents.'

'Wow!' Megan rolled her eyes. 'Sounds easier to plan a royal tour.'

Geena bit back a chuckle, going on to explain that Daniel's pin sites would need dressing three times a day. 'You'll swab round the sites with Betadine. OK?'

'Bed bath for the first week?' Megan ventured.

Geena nodded. 'And then we'll get him into the shower, using the hoist. Cover his injured legs with plastic and so on. But you know all that.'

'I want to make a really good job of this, Sister.' Megan's rather pointed little face was set in determined lines.

'It won't all rest on you, Megan,' Geena was quick to point out, 'but, certainly, if you can form an early rapport with Daniel, it will do wonders towards his general approach to his rehabilitation.'

The next few days were hectic in the extreme. Daniel had settled in or as much as he obviously intended to.

Geena gave a wry smile. The little wretch was certainly making good use of his buzzer. She went through to her office, realising that Friday had crept up on her. And her visit to Jack's farm was tomorrow. At least she thought it was. He hadn't said anything further.

Sitting at her desk, she made a face at the roster sheets. They needed a huge overhaul. People seemed to be coming and going all over the place.

'Knock, knock!'

Geena looked up as Jack poked his head round the door. 'Hi!' She moistened her lips, suddenly nervous.

'Thought we'd better make arrangements for tomorrow.' His mouth quirked slightly, as he came in and shut the door. 'Still coming?'

'If I'm still invited,' she said with a laugh.

He snorted. 'Of course you are.' Dragging up a chair, he sat next to her, stretching out his legs and tipping his head back. 'Lord, I'll be glad to see the back of this week,' he said fervently.

'Yes, it's been a bit frantic,' Geena agreed, looking through her lashes at him. He needed to relax, she thought, and for two pins she'd get up and begin massaging the tension out of his shoulders...

'What?' Jack turned his head at that moment, a glimmer of conjecture lighting his blue eyes.

'Nothing,' she said, and couldn't tear her eyes away from his. 'Are you going to give me directions to your farm, Jack?'

'Don't be nuts.' He scoffed at the idea. 'I'll come and collect you.' He pulled his legs up and folded one across his opposite knee. 'I have an early ward round. I should get to you around ninish. OK? And bring your swimmers.'

Geena looked alarmed. 'We're not swimming in the river or something, are we?'

'No,' he said with a grin. 'There's a nicely filtered pool at the house.'

CHAPTER SEVEN

WHY was she dithering like this?

Dismayed, Geena looked down at the two swimsuits on the bed. Her choice lay between the black one-piece and a fetching electric blue bikini.

'Good grief!' she muttered, snatching control and shoving the one-piece into her canvas carry bag, along with a sarong which would suffice as a cover-up after her swim, she decided, tucking the swirl of fabric on top of her swimsuit and adding a tube of sunblock.

Turning back to the mirror, she checked her appearance yet again. She was wearing lightweight jeans and a black skinny-rib top. Indecision swept her again as the doorbell pealed. Jack. Her heart racing, she hurried to open the door.

'Hello.' He smiled and pushed himself away from the railings. 'All set?'

She nodded. 'I'll just get my bag.'

'Did you remember to bring a hat?' Jack asked as they left the city limits and hit a long unbroken stretch of country road.

'Hmm, no, I didn't.' Geena looked pained.

'Not to worry.' He flicked her a grin. 'Belinda's bound to have something in her wardrobe.'

Reassured, Geena concentrated on her surroundings. So much space, she marvelled, her gaze skimming over the vast rolling plains, their midsummer brown tinge contrasting sharply with the green pockets of cultivation. Rolled bales of hay dotted the paddocks as far as the eye could see.

She turned to him, a smile on her lips. 'The hay bales look like giant cotton reels, don't they?'

'That's a good observation.' His mouth creased into an indulgent smile and his hand reached out and found her fingers. He raised them briefly to his lips. 'Happy?'

'Of course.' Geena's heart was doing a wild tango. 'It's a glorious day. Much further to Wongaree?' she managed to ask, when he gave her back her hand.

'That's our turn-off up ahead.'

Eagerly, Geena leaned forward to peer through the windscreen. 'I'll bet it's a white gate and a tree-lined drive.'

Jack laughed. 'Almost.' With a deft twist of the wheel, he sent them smoothly over the cattle grid and onto the property.

Pine trees in various stages of growth formed a line to the homestead. 'We started planting them when we were kids,' he explained, 'but over the years a few died and had to be replaced. The symmetry's not what it should be.'

The homestead was two storeys high, of old, mellowed brick, its windows facing north towards the weathered hills and the bluest mountains Geena had ever seen.

'Well, here we are,' Jack said unnecessarily, pulling to a stop in front of a double garage almost overgrown with thick purple creeper. With a flourish he cut the engine and turned to her. 'Welcome to Wongaree, Geena.'

There was a beat of silence.

'Thanks, Jack.' Her head bent, Geena hastily picked up her bag and climbed out. She followed as he led them through a wooden gate into the back yard. A slope in the lawn allowed her to see the top of a bird table. At one end in a shallow trough several small wagtails dipped and glided and dipped again.

'There's bird life here galore.' Jack followed her gaze. 'I've a family of kookaburras, too. Now, they're the real actors.' They walked up several shallow steps to the rear patio.

'Shall I see them?'

'You will if you plan to be here in the morning.'

His quiet statement alerted Geena to endless possibilities, endless outcomes of this visit. All along they'd been safely at the back of her mind and right now she just wanted them to stay there.

If only they would.

They looked at each other for a moment and then a slow smile crept over his face. 'Cup of tea?' He unlocked the door and ushered her inside.

'Oh, what a fabulous kitchen!' Geena reacted instinctively to the feeling of warmth and welcome that ran out to meet her.

Obeying an impulse, she went forward and placed her hand almost reverently on the huge old wooden table, working her fingers rhythmically across the timber, finding tiny dips and grooves in its surface and speculating about the generations who had sat here.

His arms folded, Jack watched her. 'You'll understand now why I felt so strongly about keeping all this in the family,' he said quietly.

'But your parents...' Geena shook her head. 'Didn't they want to take the furniture with them when they moved?'

He shrugged. 'New home. New furniture. Mum's happy with her new streamlined look.'

'I suppose...' Geena felt pitched back in time, imagining Jack growing up here. What wonderful childhood memories he must retain. Her gaze lifted, drifting to the blue and white mugs hanging from hooks under the wooden shelf. In glass jars above them, preserves of all kinds displayed themselves in colourful array.

She wrapped her arms around her body, her

imagination running rife, and she was smelling spices, freshly baked bread, seeing birthdays and Christmases, Jack and his siblings around this beautiful old table. A mother and a father…

'Geena?'

She blinked, startled.

Jack lifted a hand and smoothed a strand of hair from her face. 'What is it?'

Pulling back, she gave a stilted laugh and improvised quickly. 'I was just thinking what tales this old table could tell if it could talk.'

'It certainly saw some action.' Almost absently he brushed his fingertips over its scrubbed surface, as if the contact was already stirring up memories.

'It doubled as a ping-pong table on school holidays,' he said with a grin. 'When it was too wet for us to be outdoors. I can vividly remember my mother dodging in between the lot of us while she tried to prepare the meals.' His head went back on a laugh. 'We thought it was screamingly funny at the time.'

Geena chuckled. 'I suppose it wouldn't have occurred to you to curtail your game and give the poor woman a bit of help, would it?'

'No way!' He seemed shocked by the very idea. 'It was usually match point or something equally important.'

His smile left a lingering warmth in his eyes and Geena felt her heart lurch. 'I'll make some tea, shall

I?' She made a dive towards the sink and began filling the kettle.

A little bemused, Jack stood against the bench, watching her. She looked so right here, he thought, and a strange spasm seared his gut. But, then, he'd known she would...

He went to change, leaving Geena alone in the kitchen. Settle down, she told herself. You're here alone with him. So what? So everything! she sighed inwardly, taking mugs down from their hooks and setting them on the worktop.

She found scones in the freezer and placed them in the microwave to reheat. Opening the pantry, she discovered strawberry jam that looked home-made. Wonderful. What else...?

'Anything I can do?' Jack asked from the region of her shoulder.

'Oh!' Geena's hand went to her heart. 'I'm just about ready, I think. I raided the freezer and the pantry. I hope that's all right. Shall we eat on the patio? If so, we'll, um, need a tray.' She stopped for breath.

Jack seemed to be holding back laughter. 'Tray coming up,' he said.

After a cup of fragrantly brewed tea, Geena felt her equilibrium even out. Lifting the pot, she poured them both a second cup and asked, 'How do you manage such a big house, Jack? Time alone would defeat you, wouldn't it?'

He shrugged. 'I use only a fraction of the space. But you're right, and I do have home help. Helen Grant, my neighbour, comes over a couple of times a week. She's glad of the job and I'm more than happy not to have to return from the hospital to chaos.'

'From what I saw in your freezer, your Helen is a pretty good cook as well.' Geena smiled at him across the rim of her mug. She'd noticed the neatly labelled food with something like awe.

'Mmm.' Jack pushed himself back from the table and hoisted his feet onto an upturned planter. 'Helen likes to cook. I pay her extra, of course. It's all going towards her university course next year.'

He half closed his eyes and they drifted into a companionable silence. It was shattered when Geena threw herself out of her chair and ran across to the railings. 'Jack—look!' She turned to him excitedly. 'What are they? Parrots of some kind?' She pointed to where a flock of brilliantly coloured small birds had descended noisily into the back garden.

Jack stirred himself and joined her at the railings. 'They're rainbow lorikeets,' he said with an indulgent half-smile. 'They've come for the honeysuckle. Greedy little beggars.'

'Aren't they just?' Geena laughed, entranced at the sight of so many of the feathered creatures feeding as they hung at impossible angles on the trailing vine.

'They seem bossy and in command but they're easily frightened off.' Almost absently, Jack's hand came up to her nape and began stroking the soft edges of her hairline. 'Look now!' His fingers tightened briefly on her skin. 'Here's a nasty old crow to frighten the daylights out of them.'

'Poor things!' Geena leaned out over the railings as the colourful mass rose with a beat of frantic wings. She turned to Jack. 'Where will they go now?'

He shrugged. 'To the creek probably. They'll feed off some native gums, collect the nectar and pollen. Life's very predictable for our wild creatures, Geena. Not like us humans,' he added softly and gathered her into his arms.

Geena could only give a little jolt of breath as he claimed her mouth.

As though they were meant for each other, their bodies flowed together, their skin warm through their clothes.

When they stopped kissing, Geena pulled back slightly but couldn't leave the circle of his arms.

Jack knew he wanted her. His body's own response was telling him that. And he'd have to be made out of wood not to recognise Geena's answering hunger. She's so beautiful, he thought. He traced the outline of her mouth with a gentle finger. 'Stay with me tonight, Geena...'

She didn't answer. Couldn't. Jack O'Neal's lovemaking filled her with the most wondrous desire and, sooner rather than later, there'd be no way to hide it from him. But sleeping with him, that could turn out to be the biggest deal of her life. Her cautious nature held her back, warned her to take her time, tread softly.

'Jack...' She took refuge in a shaky smile. 'I like being with you. No...' She shook her head. 'I *love* being with you.'

'And I love being with you,' he said deeply. He took her face between his hands. 'I badly wanted you here last weekend, Geena.'

She favoured him with an over-bright smile. 'Well, I'm here this weekend, aren't I? Weren't you going to show me your farm?'

His mouth puckered briefly. 'If that's what you want.'

'Yes, please.'

Geena felt as though they'd passed some kind of watershed as they packed up the tray and went inside. While she loaded the dishwasher, Jack went to find her a hat. He came back with a large floppy straw, its brim swathed with a jaunty black and white scarf.

Geena raised her eyebrows. 'Rome again?'

Jack squinted at the tag still dangling from the inside brim. 'Honolulu.'

'Oh, my!' Grinning, she took it and tried it on. 'OK?' In a model-like pose, she stuck a finger under her chin and pouted prettily.

Jack growled and made a grab for her but she was too slick and ran outside, laughing.

'You'll keep, Sister Wilde,' he warned, clamping a battered bush hat on his own head.

Hand in hand, they walked through the back garden and out through the gate. 'Do you ride?' Jack asked as though the idea had only just occurred to him.

She snorted. 'Only on a merry-go-round at the Royal Easter show when I was about ten. There was no money for riding lessons when I was growing up, Jack.'

He came to a stop, his eyes narrowing on her. 'Did you mind?'

'Good grief, no!' She reached up and anchored the borrowed hat as a gust of wind threatened to dislodge it. 'I hardly mixed with kids whose aspirations extended to wanting to join a pony club. Whereas you...' She spread her arms to indicate the expanse of countryside. 'You had it all at your fingertips.'

'And largely took it for granted.'

She shrugged slightly. 'That's the nature of youth, I guess.'

They took the Jeep and went exploring.

'It's only pocket-sized acreage now, as I told you.' Jack slammed the vehicle into gear and took off to what he termed the high country. He travelled slowly, allowing Geena time to absorb her surroundings.

'How many cattle do you run?' Geena asked.

'Very few.' Jack's gaze followed hers to where his six-strong herd of Dexters stood contentedly in the shade. 'Just a few to make it feel like home.'

'No sheep?'

'God, no!' His mouth pulled back in a grimace. 'I hate sheep.'

She chuckled. 'Because they have to be—?'

'Crutched,' he supplied heavily. 'This is as far as we go.' He eased the Jeep into a U-turn so that they were looking down on the rolling plains below.

'Oh, yes...' Geena breathed out on a little sigh. She got slowly out of the Jeep and looked about her.

'Let's sit over here.' As if it now seemed the most natural thing in the world to be touching her, Jack slid his arm around her waist and guided her across to a huge gum tree and a grassy patch of shade beneath.

'No wonder you came back,' Geena said softly, pulling her knees up to her chin and lowering her gaze to the curve of shimmering water of the lagoon and the carpet of water lilies that covered its surface. 'It's special, isn't it?'

'Like you.' Jack's voice was muted. In an abrupt movement, he tipped her hat off and bent to her, placing soft, sweet kisses on her temple, her cheek, the tiny beauty spot at the side of her mouth. 'Geena...'

Geena felt a sudden strange lightness. Love and desire rolled into one wild surge, sweeping through her body and out to the tips of her fingers and toes.

In a skilful rearrangement of muscles, Jack eased her back against him, his arms forming a cradle for her slenderness. With a feeling of rightness, she curled her body into his, each curve and hollow finding a home, a placement as though they'd been carved out, and were waiting to be filled.

Overlapping his hands around her waist, he nuzzled a kiss into her hair. 'Life looks pretty good from this angle, doesn't it?'

Geena turned, her heart in her eyes. 'Yes,' she agreed softly, realising that to have said anything else would have been a lie.

Without letting go of her, he inched back so that he had the support of the tree trunk. Taking his cue, she nestled against him and there seemed no urgency to talk. Only to be.

For a long time they did little else other than absorb their surroundings, the dappled sunlight, the pungent scent of hay-making, the drone of the farm tractors.

'Hey!' Jack gave her a little shake. 'Fancy a swim before lunch?'

Back at the house, he showed her into Belinda's bedroom and she changed into her black swimsuit. Her heart was thrumming as she made her way downstairs.

Following the haunting sound of a Roberta Flack recording, she unlatched a lattice gate and joined Jack at the poolside. 'I love her music.' Geena tossed her sarong onto a nearby lounger.

Jack lifted his head and met her eyes over the tapedeck. His eyes glowed with appreciation. 'Ready to hit the water?' He arched a dark brow at her and she nodded, following him into the pool with a clean, neat dive.

They swam, stroking lazily up and down the pool, and then they floated. Blinking the droplets away from her eyes, Geena looked up into the canopy of blue sky—beautiful, vast. A feeling of pure gladness twisted inside her.

The beauty of the world was all around her, Jack was barely an arm's length away and nothing had ever felt so right.

I love him, she thought, almost giddy with the realisation. Suddenly she wanted to share everything with him—the sky, the cool depth of the water, the sharp tang of the eucalypts and the other more elusive smells that charged her senses, almost bringing her to tears of joy.

'Jack?' Scooping a hand into the water, she scattered droplets onto his chest. 'Open your eyes.'

'Hmm?'

'What do you see?' Her voice was hushed with expectancy.

'Not a lot.' Shading his eyes, he squinted into the sunlight. 'A great dollop of sky,' he observed wryly. 'Could be a storm later.'

'Peasant!' She made a lunge at him but he was too quick. He ducked her and she came up slicked with water, her hands clasped around his neck. Laughing, they kissed playfully, once, twice.

Just when it changed into something else Geena wasn't sure. With a deep exhalation of breath Jack laid his open palm across her stomach and her heart thudded faster as he bent and kissed the soft swell of her breast just visible above her suit's neckline.

'Jack...' Her hands slid down the wet sleekness of his back and he dragged in a huge breath and lifted his head.

'Out, I think, Geena.' His voice was a bit hoarse and he shook the water from his hair. Towing her to the side of the pool, he hoisted her up and onto the decking.

'Coming?' Geena bent and held out a hand to him.

'In a minute.' His grin was rueful. 'Have to get myself in order first.'

If being in love made you this hungry, then she would have to watch her diet. Geena almost skipped around the big kitchen as she threw together a green salad for lunch. Jack was outside barbecuing the steaks.

She took a mouthful of wine from the glass beside her and smiled almost guiltily. She didn't need wine. She was drunk from happiness already.

'Lunch was wonderful,' Geena said some time later as she lifted the coffee-pot and poured them both a cup. 'I was ravenous.'

'I noticed.' Jack hurriedly wiped the grin off his face as their eyes locked.

Geena felt herself blushing and showed him the tip of her tongue. Happy didn't even begin to describe how she felt. 'Jack?' Under the outdoor table her bare toes nudged his. 'How long were you married?'

His head jerked up as if she'd activated a string. 'You push the darnedest buttons sometimes, Sister Wilde.'

Geena was taken aback. 'Is the subject taboo?'

'No... I suppose not.' His head went back against the cushioned rest and he looked out across the pool and into the distance. He knew he should talk about it and Geena was the least judgemental person he knew but his gut tightened at the thought of her reaction.

He wiped a hand across his jaw. 'I guess I should be getting on with my life. Better than I have been...'

'Sometimes you have to go back before you can move forward.' Geena's eyes met his with a faint challenge across the rim of her coffee-cup.

'Pearls of wisdom, Geena?'

'I'm full of them.' She gave him another nudge. 'How long were you married?'

He lifted a hand and pushed it through his hair. 'Zoe and I were married just over two years—as you'd probably say, not long enough to have given it our best shot.'

Geena ignored the small jibe. 'Where did you meet?'

'Would you believe at a ball at the Sydney Opera House? Mutual friends introduced us. I'd just joined the staff at St Vincent's. Zoe was in town especially for a photo shoot. She was a model,' he clarified. 'Not on the catwalk. She did photographic work, high-quality sexy stuff for a cosmetic company.'

Just as well I don't suffer from my ego, Geena thought wryly, listening intently as Jack began speaking again.

'There's not much to tell really,' he stalled. 'We got married. We got divorced.'

Geena clicked her tongue. 'That's not telling me anything, Jack. Were you in love to begin with?'

He snorted. 'What's love? OK...' He held up a hand. 'We thought we were, I suppose. On reflection it was all perhaps just too physical to last. Or maybe our lifestyles were to blame. I know our work schedules were crazy. We hardly saw each other some weeks.'

Geena watched as he tugged off a citrus leaf and began shredding it with his thumb and forefinger.

'Just after our second wedding anniversary, Zoe got pregnant. It wasn't planned. Nevertheless, I was ecstatic. Zoe was less than happy about the prospect of motherhood.'

'Perhaps she was worried about losing her figure?' Geena was determined to be fair.

He shrugged. 'I think she just hated the whole idea. She had a modelling commitment to meet in Europe, a chance to audition for a TV soap in Sydney. No.' He gave a bitter laugh. 'She wasn't happy at all.'

'Oh, Jack.' Geena entwined her fingers in his, squeezing them gently, giving him wordless comfort.

'If the pregnancy had been straightforward, we might have coped. But she had hellish morning sickness. Nothing seemed to work, at least not long enough for her to get on with her life. She was bored, miserable, so angry.'

'With you?'

'Of course, with me. Eventually, I took matters into my own hands. I began by asking my boss for a decent work roster and I told Zoe to rest and I'd do everything.'

Geena blinked. 'Did that work?'

He shrugged and looked broodingly into the distance. 'For a while. Until the day I'd forgotten to exchange her videos. She decided she couldn't wait until I'd got home. She took her car and went to the shops. She was feeling ill, decided to give her seat belt a miss…'

'Oh, heavens…' Geena gave a little shudder. She just knew what was coming.

He nodded. 'She wasn't badly hurt but shocked to blazes. She lost the baby that night.'

Geena went perfectly still. 'You blamed her, didn't you?'

'You bet I did.' His voice grated harshly. 'I did a real number on her.'

'Jack, how could you?' Geena's voice held stunned disbelief.

'I was out of my head. Stressed beyond my limits. But it was no excuse. I should've been able to comfort my own wife—but I couldn't.' His throat worked as he swallowed. 'We more or less made up but it didn't work.'

He picked up her hand and turned it over. 'The day we looked at each other and realised there was nothing left was the worst day of my life. We split. I think she's in the States somewhere. Still modelling.'

'And you're here,' Geena said quietly.

'Yes. I'm here.'

For Geena the rest of the day passed in a kind of vacuum. Jack had gone into one of his quiet moods, half-heartedly digging out old scrapbooks and photos from his youth at Geena's insistence. She sensed his preoccupation and tried gently to draw him out, but it was as if his thoughts were trapped elsewhere and she could gain no admittance.

When it was dusk he took her to see his wombats but even they were tardy and refused to come out of their burrows.

Jack was clearly disappointed. 'They're usually out and about now,' he said. 'They sense the darkness like clockwork.'

'From inside their burrows?' Geena looked puzzled, moving closer to him so that their arms were touching.

'Their instinct is amazing.' He hunkered down, taking her with him. 'They have a kind of little viewing station at the entrance to their burrow and from there they can judge the outside temperature and light conditions before they venture out.'

Geena was impressed. 'Perhaps they'll come out for me next time?' she said, as they turned away from the enclosure and began making their way slowly back to the house.

Jack didn't answer.

They went in through the back gate again and Geena collected her swimmers and towel from the clothesline where she'd hung them to dry.

'I don't think it will storm after all.' She tried to make conversation as they went inside. In the kitchen she looked around, as if trying to take something tangible from the day. It all looked the same, smelled the same, but something had changed in the atmosphere.

No, it hadn't. She shook her head silently. It was the atmosphere between her and Jack that had changed. She jumped as he touched her arm.

'If you'd like to get your things together, I'll take you home now.'

His words struck her as painfully as fists and she swallowed the hurt with a stiff little smile.

What price now her assumption he'd been about to ask her once more to stay the night? It was as clear as the nose on her face that she was the last thing on his mind.

CHAPTER EIGHT

ON SUNDAY Geena went through the motions. She cleaned her flat and then prepared to spend a frustratingly long time in the laundramat because her washing machine refused to do the job she'd programmed it for.

'Modern technology!' she fumed, gathering up her sheets and towels, her uniforms and sundry other things and bundling them into the boot of her car.

As she shot out of the carport she thought grimly that the pioneer women's wood-fired wash coppers would never have let them down like this. But, then, it had taken most of every Monday to complete the family's laundry, she reflected, a chink of humour lightening her mood.

The phone was ringing when she got home, staggering through the door with her clean laundry. Jack? Dumping the bags on the floor, she lunged at the phone.

'Geena? It's Cassie.'

'Oh, Cass. Hi.' Geena's heart crept back to its rightful place and resumed an even beat. 'What's up?'

'Do you have any plans for this afternoon?'

Geena's eyes went towards the two bags of neatly folded laundry. 'Nothing I can't bear to postpone,' she said wryly. 'Did you want to do something?'

'Actually, I wanted your input.' Cassie laughed. 'I'm being married in less than two months and I haven't decided on a style for my dress yet.'

Geena knew what was coming and decided to head if off. 'Cass, if I have to look through another bride magazine this side of Christmas, I'll tear my hair out.'

Cassie chuckled. 'I'd forgotten both your sisters were married last year. Big drama about choosing the gear, was there?'

'Like you wouldn't believe,' Geena said feelingly.

'OK.' Cassie was good-natured. 'What about a movie, then? There's a comedy showing, I think.'

Geena ran a finger along the phone cord. She could certainly do with a laugh. But what if Jack called? She hardened her heart. He could damned well call again! 'OK, Cass. I'd love to. What time?'

'Four o'clock. Perhaps we can go for a bite afterwards?'

'Brad let you down today?' There was a smile in Geena's voice.

'Helping his dad,' Cassie returned cryptically. 'They're baling hay.'

Geena laughed. 'Oh, well, if you must marry a farmer.'

'Grazier, darling!' Cassie used her posh voice. 'Do you mind?'

'My mistake. See you at four.' Geena put the phone down with a little chuckle. At least the movie would fill some of the day. Besides which, Cassie was always good fun.

There was no message from Jack when she got home just after nine. Not that she'd expected one. He'd left her with barely a word last night. Tossing her keys on to the coffee-table, she went through to the bedroom.

She began organising her clothes for work, thinking she could probably do it in her sleep by now. Perhaps she'd been in nursing too long. She pondered the question as she buffed up her navy shoes. Was that the reason she was almost dreading the ward tomorrow? No, it was facing Jack she was dreading. A stab of pain and trepidation ambushed her unexpectedly and she sighed. Why couldn't she have fallen in love with someone less complicated? And that, she decided ruefully, was about as futile as asking why pigs didn't fly.

Placing her shoes neatly side by side, she went into the bathroom to wash her hands. She flicked a glance in the mirror and grimaced. She hadn't slept properly last night. If tonight was no better, she'd be lucky not to end up with huge dark circles the size of dinner plates under her eyes...

The ping of the doorbell sent her hand to her throat, warm colour creeping up her face. Jack?

She ran to open the door.

It was raining on Monday morning. Geena looked out at the landscape and thought wryly it was the kind of steady drizzle that would have the farmers smiling and the mothers of school kids dredging up an endless supply of patience.

She was running late, preoccupied, a dozen things running through her mind. She drove her car to work and then wondered why she'd bothered as the hospital car park looked overflowing at the seams already.

Circling the precincts for a second time, she got lucky and slid her Mazda hatchback neatly into a just-vacated space.

She read the signs that it was going to be one of those days as soon as she walked on to the ward. Within seconds she was swamped.

The night sister had gone home sick and her deputy was less than on top of things. Geena frowned over the report.

There had been another whooping-cough admission, this time a three-year-old, Madeleine Graham. The little one's high temperature had brought on a fit. She'd fitted a second time and Jack had been called in. He'd given valium IV and the child had settled. She was still on oxygen, asleep but rousable.

Twins had been admitted with stomachaches for further investigation. Geena stroked her forehead in concentration. There was also a child with concussion after a fall from a swing and a two-year-old boy who had run onto hot coals at a family picnic over the weekend. Jack would decide whether the toddler would need to be transferred to a children's burns unit in Sydney later in the day.

Geena sighed as she checked the theatre list. Three grommet procedures were scheduled. Two children had arrived, one hadn't shown. She'd have to phone.

She'd need to phone the agency as well. Piers wouldn't be in. She lifted the phone, hoping the supervisor would approve a replacement to cover the shift.

Somewhere along the line she had to speak to Jack, but that obviously wouldn't be possible for a while. He'd left word he was attending a meeting elsewhere in the city.

Toni was holding the fort and, Geena thought, looking pretty glum about it. By rights the young resident should have been off duty. Geena's mouth firmed. She wholeheartedly supported the current inquiry by the AMA into the long hours being worked by junior doctors in hospitals.

'Sister, could I speak to you, please?'

Geena was in her office, sifting through a sea of computer printouts, when Megan popped her head round the door.

'Certainly.' Geena waved the student to a chair and pushed her paperwork to one side. 'What is it, Megan?'

'Daniel DeVere is acting like a two-year-old.'

The disgust in the junior's voice made Geena hold back a smile. 'Since when?'

'The last few days. As you know, he's left-handed.' Megan leaned forward, her expression earnest. 'And with his arm in plaster, he's got to manage with his right.'

'But you're cutting his food up, aren't you?'

'Of course.' The junior nurse pulled a face. 'But surely he can manage to hold a piece of toast without me having to cut into soldiers!'

Geena kept her face straight with difficulty. 'How's the mum?'

'More hindrance than help.' Megan shrugged. 'Determined to do every little thing for him.'

'It sometimes happens like that.' Geena saw the third-year out. 'Leave it with me. I'll sort something out to try to make life a bit easier for you. Everything else OK?'

Megan nodded. 'Yes, thanks.'

Geena heaved a sigh of relief. For once, the paperwork made sense, saving her precious minutes and more phone calls. She went back on the ward, almost colliding with Phil Carter as he edged backwards out of the treatment room.

'Hi, Geena.' He put out a hand to steady her. 'Monday got you by the throat, too?'

'You could say that.' Her mouth lifted in a wry smile.

'Anything I can do for you?' His grey eyes were kind.

Geena took a deep breath. 'Perhaps...' She filled him in about the DeVeres.

'Kid being a pain in the butt, is he?'

'It's not the easiest time for him,' Geena said sympathetically. 'And, unfortunately, his mum is aggravating the situation by treating him like a baby.'

'Ah!' Phil's fair head went back in comprehension. 'Want me to do a spot of PR? See if that helps?'

'Would you? I thought Mrs DeVere was going to be sensible but he's their only child...'

'Leave it to me.' He grinned. 'I'm usually real good with the parents. Comes of being one myself.'

Another nice man, Geena thought, watching him amble off towards Daniel's room.

She looked at her watch and frowned. Where the hell are you, Jack?

She spotted him shortly after when he spilled from the lift with the first visitors.

'Jack...' She had almost to sprint to catch up with him as he strode towards his office.

He jerked to a stop. 'Yes, Sister. What is it?'

She swallowed. He looked stressed and not over-thrilled to see her. 'I need to speak to you,' she said hesitantly.

His jaw tightened. 'If it's personal, it'll have to wait.'

Geena froze. He may as well have struck her. 'It's a staff matter,' she said coolly.

'Medical staff?' His brows met in a frown.

Geena shook her head. 'Nursing staff, actually.'

He took a step and half turned. 'That's your domain, Sister. Not mine.'

She stared at him, stunned. His attitude was rude if not downright dismissive. 'I wouldn't ask if it weren't important.'

He let his breath out on a harsh sigh. 'All right. Come into my office.'

Tight-lipped, Geena followed and waited while he closed the door.

Jack went to his side of the desk, hooking his jacket over the back of his chair. 'I've a lot on my plate today,' he said shortly. 'Could you be quick?'

Geena's chin came up. 'Could we possibly sit down?'

He shrugged as if it didn't matter one way or the other. Nevertheless, he sank into his chair, folded his arms and looked at her.

Dear God, what was the matter with him? Geena's stomach turned upside down. But she was fighting for something here. She met his gaze determinedly. 'Piers Korda came to see me last night. He was very upset. Tasha has miscarried.'

'Oh, hell…' Jack's voice was like gravel. 'That's tough. How far along was she?'

Geena felt the rush of tears to her eyes. 'Just on twelve weeks.'

He swore softly. 'Is Piers taking some time off?'

Geena shrugged. 'Only enough to put Tasha on a plane to her parents this afternoon.'

'That's no good,' he said harshly. 'They need to grieve together. Otherwise…' He ran a hand roughly through his hair. 'Was she admitted here?'

'Mercy. Piers was collecting her this morning.'

'When did it happen?'

'Some time on Saturday.' Geena bit her lip. 'She had a D and C. Jack…' She placed both hands on the desk and appealed to him. 'They're not coping at all. Could you talk to them?'

He stared at her, his eyes unblinking. 'No, Geena. I'm afraid I can't.'

'But you've been there!' she cried, ignoring the obvious strain behind his words. 'They need help.'

'There are qualified counsellors for that,' he said, his voice flat.

'They're not about to listen to *strangers*.' Geena's hand curled into a small fist against her heart. 'They need a friend, Jack, someone who knows what they're going through.' She blinked. 'Piers is afraid Tasha will go to her parents and not come back.'

Jack moved restively in his chair. 'They're close, aren't they? They'll work it out.'

Geena swallowed. 'But not before they've put each other through needless heartache. Piers says she won't even talk to him about losing the baby…'

'Where's her head?' Jack squeezed a hand against his eyes. 'It's not her sole prerogative to be hurting. Her husband's grief is just as real. It was *his* child, too, for crying out loud!'

'Then you'll go and see them?' Geena clasped her hands together in a plea.

'Geena, my own experience was not the same. Zoe and I were poles apart even before she lost the baby.'

'But at least you know how it felt! Please, Jack…' Geena's eyes were entreating.

'No.' His throat worked as he swallowed. 'I can't go around offering people happy endings. I wouldn't even begin to try.'

'I see…' Geena got slowly to her feet and placed her hands across the back of the chair. She looked at him a little sadly. 'I thought you were the one person who could've helped, Jack. Obviously I was wrong. But, then, I seem to have made rather a lot of rash assumptions lately.' With her head high, she turned on her heel and walked out.

'Dammit!' Jack picked up the nearest object, which happened to be his diary, and threw it against the wall.

'I don't need this!' His teeth clamped on the muttered words. In an abrupt movement he hunched over his desk, pushing his hands roughly through his hair.

He gave a hollow laugh. He certainly didn't need Geena's big brown eyes looking at him as though he'd just crawled out from under a log!

Geena went straight to the staffroom. She felt shaken beyond belief at Jack's response. Blindly, her fingers clumsy and uncooperative, she managed to get herself a mug of coffee and then stood, her hands clasped around its warmth, peering out into the rain.

Her mind felt numb, unable to comprehend the change in him since Saturday. Dear heaven! Saturday and all they'd done came ripping back in vivid colour and she gulped down the rest of her coffee.

'Anyone home?' Cassie's smooth auburn head came shooting round the door. 'I was told I might find you in here. I'm on the borrow.'

'Cass.' Geena turned and blinked and came back to reality with a thud. 'What do you need?' She stepped to the sink and rinsed her mug.

'You mean apart from a few days off?' Cassie slid a gingernut biscuit from its just-opened packet and began to crunch it with obvious enjoyment. 'Would you believe we've run out of nappies?' She made a face. 'We've a suspected gastro. Little bub's running through nappies like wildfire.'

'Didn't you get your supply form the laundry?' Geena asked as they made their way back to the station.

Cassie grinned. 'Slip-up, I'm afraid. Now they can't get any to us until mid-afternoon.'

They went into the treatment room which also housed the linen trolley. 'I'll return them as soon as we get our supply,' Cassie promised.

Geena shrugged. 'No hurry. We've usually got heaps. Perhaps we'll see your little one up here later?'

'Hmm...maybe not. Mary's hoping it won't be necessary to admit him. The mum was pretty prompt, getting him in to us before he got too dehydrated and so on.'

They stepped back into the ward just as Jack strode past, his jacket looped over one shoulder on his way to the lift.

Cassie raised an eyebrow. 'Where's he off to in such an almighty hurry?'

'Hopefully, out to play in the traffic,' Geena said darkly.

'Oh, dear.' Cassie sucked in her bottom lip. 'Lovers' tiff?'

'We're not lovers,' Geena gritted. 'Nor likely to be. And at the moment I'd say we're not even friends.'

'Oh, drat.' Cassie backed against the wall, juggling her linen packs against her chest. 'And there I was thinking you and Jack would be the next ones down the aisle after Brad and me.'

Geena clicked her tongue. 'Don't be ridiculous, Cassie! I've never even hinted at such a thing.'

'No?' Cassie raised a finely etched eyebrow. 'You only dropped his name about a zillion times into the conversation last night.'

'I did not!'

'Ducky, you did.' Cassie's eyes were alight with amusement. 'Besides,' she said smugly. 'I've seen you dancing together. I couldn't have got a cigarette paper between you.'

'Very cute!' Geena rolled her eyes. 'It was slow dancing not rock and roll.'

'I know.' Cassie almost purred. 'Nice, wasn't it? Keep me posted.' She went off chuckling, leaving Geena feeling as though she was coming slowly unstuck.

For the next hour she deliberately made herself busy, calling in on the schoolroom, the play room and stopping to have a game of ludo with one of the twins, now bubbling over with normality.

Appendicitis had been ruled out and Phil had cleared her to go home with her sister later in the day.

The two young grommit patients were back from Theatre and sharing a room. Geena went to check on their progress. They were both grizzly and out of sorts, their respective mothers hovering anxiously.

Geena checked the charts with a professional eye. 'Your boys are doing really well,' she said, favouring each parent with a warm smile.

'I hope this will stop Callum getting those awful ear infections again.' The mother of one of the children was trying to pacify him with his favourite teddy bear.

Geena made sure both drips were still in place. 'Dr O'Neal indicated it would, didn't he?'

'Well, yes.' The mother nodded. 'He didn't do the operation, though, did he?'

'No.' Geena's lashes fluttered down and lifted. 'He wasn't in Theatre today. But he will be doing rounds later,' she added, her voice carefully expressionless.

'Geena, I've had an idea!' Krista caught up with Geena as she hurried back to her office.

'Better run it past me, then.' Geena drummed up a faint smile and they went inside. 'Take a pew, Kris.'

'It's about Tasha and Piers.' The junior RN sat

down with a plonk. 'I thought it might be nice if we sent them some flowers to cheer them up.'

Geena felt a stab of guilt. She should have thought of it herself but she'd been off on a different tack, trying to get help for the couple in a more practical way. And that hadn't even got to first base, had it?

'That's a terrific idea, Kris.' Geena rearranged a couple of things on her desktop. 'But we'd better be quick. Tasha's booked on a flight to Sydney this afternoon.'

'That's where her family lives, isn't it?' The younger woman looked thoughtful. 'Poor old Piers. Couldn't he have got time off to go too?'

Geena felt tears at the back of her throat again. How much should she tell Krista or how little? Geena had thought it wise to inform their team about Tasha's miscarriage, mostly because she hadn't wanted Piers to have to field any awkward questions when he returned to work. Geena bit her lip. Last night his defences had seemed on the brink of crumbling. 'I gather they've sorted something out between them.' She skirted round Krista's query with a little shrug. 'Now, about these flowers.'

'Oh, yes.' Krista leaned forward, an obvious organisational gleam in her eyes. 'I thought cut flowers. Something really huge and bright.'

Geena nodded. 'That sounds wonderful.'

'I'll order them from Bouquets and Blossoms,'

Krista said. 'Their stuff is fabulous. Bit expensive but worth it. And they'll deliver within the hour. Or,' she said consideringly, 'I could pick them up personally and whizz them round to the Kordas' in my lunch-break.'

'Kris, that's probably not a great idea,' Geena said carefully. 'I imagine they're still at sixes and sevens a bit just now.'

'And I come waltzing in with flowers.' Krista made an apologetic small face. 'Yes,' she agreed. 'Much better we send them.' She squinted at her watch. 'Should I do a whip-around, then?'

'No, that'll take ages.' Geena delved into a draw for her wallet. 'Get them on my credit card. We'll settle up later.'

'Oh, Geena!' Krista took the plastic with a happy grin. 'That's really sweet of you. I'll think up something really meaningful to say on the card as well,' she promised.

'I'm sure you will.' Geena laughed a little drily. 'Your entrepreneurial skills are becoming legendary.'

'Really?' Krista's gaze dropped modestly.

'Really,' Geena echoed. 'Make your phone call from here.' She touched the other woman's shoulder. 'I'm going to take an early lunch-break.'

CHAPTER NINE

BY THE time Geena left the hospital at the end of her shift, the rain had cleared, leaving the sky a pale wash of blue and the air still and hot.

She decided to go for a swim in the pool at the sports centre, and no matter how many laps it took she'd slough off the effects of one of the roughest days of her life.

Momentarily, her hands tightened on the steering-wheel. Except for accompanying Jack on his ward round, her contact with him during the afternoon had been professional and minimal.

Would it be the same again tomorrow? And the day after? She suppressed a shiver. Surely she wasn't such a rotten judge of character, was she?

She felt relaxed after her swim but the flat seemed airless and depressing when she returned. Flicking on the overhead fan, she went through methodically opening windows and then threw herself under the shower.

Half-dry and wrapped in a fluffy towel, she plonked herself down on the bedroom stool and stared in the mirror.

It was almost dark when Geena stirred herself. Switching on the make-up light, she grimaced. Her hair had dried flatly against her head and she'd have to get up earlier than usual in the morning and try to do something with it before she went to work.

Almost absently she pulled on shorts and a brief top and went through to the kitchen, automatically folding back the louvred door panels that opened onto the little courtyard. She took a step out into the garden. It was flooded with soft darkness, the faint ripple of her wind chimes the only sound in the stillness.

Geena ended the long letter to her mother and glanced at the clock on the mantlepiece. Nine-thirty. She blocked a yawn and stretched. Just time for a cup of tea, she decided, and then bed.

She made the tea and took it out into the courtyard. Sitting in one of the canvas director's chairs, she turned her gaze up to the night sky.

It was a long time before she registered the ringing of the doorbell. Piers... She closed her eyes for a moment. She didn't really want to talk to him now... Sighing, she put down her cup and walked slowly inside, reaching the front door just as the bell rang sharply once more.

Snatching the door open, she ran her eyes over the male figure in battered jeans and loose white shirt standing there. 'Hello, Jack,' she said, relieved at how detached she felt.

'Where were you?' he demanded edgily.

'What do you want?' she countered with a distinct lack of enthusiasm.

He shifted from one foot to the other. 'I want to talk to you.'

Involuntarily her fingers curled around the doorknob. 'I'm not sure I want to listen to anything you have to say at the moment.'

His head came up sharply and he rammed his hands into his back pockets. 'What about an apology?'

Geena made a resigned little gesture with her hand and turned back into the room. The front door closed quietly behind Jack, and he followed her through to the kitchen.

'I've just boiled the water for tea,' she said. 'Would you like a cup?'

'Sounds good.' He moved closer to her.

Very aware of him beside her, Geena got down one of her bright yellow mugs. She gnawed gently at her bottom lip. He seemed ill at ease; there was an air of vulnerability about him. Tough. She hardened her heart. After what he'd put her through today, he deserved to feel insecure.

She forced herself to meet his eyes and her heart turned to marshmallow. 'Have you eaten?'

'Yes, thanks.' He took the mug a bit awkwardly.

Geena swallowed the sudden lump in her throat. Drat the man! He was getting to her all over again. 'I'm in the courtyard,' she said, and he followed her outside, sitting opposite her. Geena curled her legs back under the chair. No way was she going to risk even the slightest accidental contact with him.

'I'm sorry about my boorish behaviour today, Geena.' He hunched over his mug. 'It was juvenile and pathetic.'

Geena couldn't have agreed more. She dragged in a deep breath. 'I did wonder what I'd done to deserve it,' she said quietly.

His mouth straightened into a hard line. 'I don't understand it myself. It's complicated—'

'It isn't really, Jack.' Geena had come to a few conclusions herself. Lifting her mug, she took a careful mouthful of her tea. 'Everything changed after you told me about Zoe—and the baby. You changed,' she emphasised with a little shrug. 'And I think right then you began to resent me because I'd pressed you to talk about your marriage. Confront things you'd much rather have left alone…'

His eyes narrowed in conjecture, as if it hadn't occurred to him that she might have placed her own interpretation on his odd behaviour. His lips curled. 'Turned philosopher now, have we, Geena?'

She flushed. 'I'm a nurse, Jack. I evaluate people and circumstances all the time.' It just took longer when she couldn't be objective. She swallowed the tears clogging her throat. Did he realise how much he'd hurt her? Probably not. She looked down at her hands. 'Perhaps you need to see someone. To talk it all through…'

'I have.'

Bewildered, shaken, she just stared at him.

'I went to see Piers and Tasha.'

'Oh…' Geena's voice was a thread. And then she remembered his flight from the hospital while she and Cassie had all but joked about it. Oh, Jack! She put her hands to her cheeks and felt the dampness there. But she had to ask. 'Did it help?'

'Yes.' His voice roughened and he turned his face towards her. 'It helped.'

With a little cry Geena leapt from her chair and right onto his knee. And he was waiting for her. His arms came round her, held her and held her. For the longest time.

Finally Geena stirred. She lifted a hand and touched his cheek. 'Are Piers and Tasha all right now?'

Jack tightened his arms around her. 'Time will tell, but they seem to be. At least Tasha cancelled her flight to Sydney. They decided to have a few days up the coast instead. And Piers said to tell you to roster him for work as from next Monday.'

'Better and better.' Geena sat up but he tugged her down again. 'Will Tasha come back to work, do you think?'

'Mmm, probably.' He nuzzled a kiss on her

throat. 'When she's feeling emotionally strong again.'

'We've really missed her.' Geena stroked her thumb across his knuckles. 'She could get even the tardiest kids to enjoy their physio. She has a real gift. I hope they'll be able to have another baby...'

Jack touched his fingertips to her bare midriff, making her shiver. 'You like everything right with the world, don't you, Geena?'

'So?' she hedged. 'What's wrong with that?'

'Nothing.' A slightly teasing smile was playing around his mouth. 'It's a lovely trait.'

His blue gaze captured hers. Even in the dim light she could feel its intensity. She swallowed drily.

'How about you, Jack? How are you feeling?'

She felt the sigh go right through him.

'Wiped out. A bit empty.' His head rolled towards her. 'I feel so badly about hurting you...' Sliding his hand beneath her top, he cupped her breast, feeling its fullness as though driven by the need to reconnect, to feel her warmth, her femininity. 'I thought I'd lost you!' His tortured little confession brought a soft denial from Geena's lips.

She trailed her fingers from his mouth to his throat. 'I'm a survivor, remember? I need you Jack.'

His arms closed even more tightly about her. 'I need *you*, Geena. As much as my own breathing.'

She burrowed against him. 'Will you stay?'

'Please...'

Before Geena could catch her breath, his mouth was on hers, hungry, urgent, seeking possession with a longing that would not be denied any longer.

'About this bed of yours.' Jack's tone was mock-serious as they closed the louvred doors and locked them. 'Just how big is it?'

'Big enough.' Geena felt a rush of emotion but with it came certainty. She loved this man and being with him mattered more than anything else ever had in the whole of her life.

'I need a lot of room,' he cautioned, hooking his arm around her shoulders.

They took the few steps to her bedroom.

'You'll have a lot of room,' she said with lover-like indulgence. 'It's queen-size.'

'Hmm. Don't know if I like the sound of that.' He muffled the words into her neck.

'Jack...' Her laugh was fractured, nerves gripping her insides like tentacles.

'That's me.' He lowered his arm and caught her close to his side.

Geena felt her teeth chattering. He was being light-hearted for a purpose and she loved him all the more for it.

They entered the half-darkened bedroom. Stopped.

'Jack...' She turned in the circle of his arms. 'I...haven't done this for a while.'

'Me neither.' He smoothed back a strand of hair from her temple, his expression tenderly concerned. 'Perhaps we can support each other.'

She stifled a giggle. 'You make it sound as though we're both on walking-frames.'

'Now, there's a challenge,' he said softly, drawing his index finger down her throat to the soft curve of her breast. 'How about we just let it happen?' His voice was low, husky with promise.

Geena swallowed. 'I'd like that too...'

As if he had been waiting for just such an invitation, he lifted her right up off her feet and gathered her in.

The big bed welcomed them, the sheets cool against their skin. The moonlight through the jasmine that clung in strands outside the window cast silken shadows across their limbs.

Geena moved slowly, as if in a dream, placing her hand over his as it shaped her breast.

Above her Jack's eyes were shot to silver pinpoints of desire, his breathing uneven.

'You're beautiful...' He stroked down her outflung arm to her hip. 'I want you, Geena.' His voice came out on a long sigh. 'More than you'll ever know.'

Geena half raised her head and he bent to meet her and their lips joined. A spark, bright and clear, ignited, enveloping her, and she knew they had arrived at that moment when all is trust. *I love you.* The three little words echoed in her heart and she abandoned herself into his care.

She woke for no good reason. At once memories flooded her mind and she stretched out a hand to touch him. But he wasn't there.

'Jack?'

'I'm here.' He ambled into the bedroom.

'Oh.' Pure relief shot through her. Struggling upright, she dragged the sheet up to her chin. 'I thought you'd gone.'

'I'm just about to.' He came over to the bed and parked himself on the edge next to her. 'I was looking for something to write you a note.' His eyes crinkled down at her. 'Good morning...' He bent and pressed his mouth to the side of her throat.

'Yes.' She flushed. 'I mean, good morning to you, too.' She took an uncertain breath. 'Do you have to get home to your animals?'

'That also. But I need some clothes. I've a breakfast meeting with the mayor.'

She looked at him, absorbing the lines of his face, the fine texture of his skin. 'What's happening?'

He knuckled her cheek. 'If I can pull the right strings, a mass inoculation for the kids without protection.'

'Against whooping cough?' She rubbed her cheek against his hand.

'Mmm. Derek and I are combining with some of the GPs to try to get a programme up and running. It'll need co-operation from the parents and schools, of course. We had a meeting yesterday and it was decided we tackle the local council first and then through them, hopefully, the state health department.'

Geena wrinkled her nose. 'Are you good at cutting through red tape, Jack?'

'I've had my moments. Geena...' He reached out to touch her hair, curving his hand so that his thumb brushed along the side of her face. 'I have to go.'

'I'll, um, see you at work, then,' she said in a voice suddenly turned husky. She licked her lips, wondering where they stood now. But this was not the time to ask him.

He turned at the door, a slow-burning heat in the look he sent her. 'Last night was wonderful, Geena. We managed quite well, didn't you think?'

'We did.' She flushed prettily. 'Despite the walking-frames.' They exchanged a grin and Geena was still smiling long after he'd gone.

CHAPTER TEN

BY WEEK'S end Geena was beginning to wonder if she'd dreamt that she and Jack had become lovers.

She'd hardly seen him. And yesterday he'd left for Sydney to have talks with the respective government ministers for health and education.

She swept used linen off the treatment couch and shoved it into the bin. If they could get the programme going, it would be wonderful. Anything to stop those poor little kids coughing their hearts out.

Her look turned wry. If anyone could make it happen, Jack could. When he got his teeth into something, he went all the way. Her thoughts grew soft and she wondered if he'd been a determined small boy, hellbent on achieving.

Perhaps she'd have the opportunity of asking his mother one day. Her heart twisted painfully. That thought opened up a whole new dimension to their relationship and Geena had never been any good at foretelling the future.

She stood for a moment stunned by the power of the sensations that coursed through her. Could she and Jack have a future together...?

'Postcard from Piers and Natasha.' Diane Lewis popped her head around the door. She waggled the card with its bright blue seascape. 'I'll stick it on the noticeboard in the staffroom.'

'Thanks, Di.' Geena smiled. 'Are they having a good time?'

'Secm to be.' The receptionist grinned. 'Piers says Tasha's teaching him how to fish.'

Geena chuckled. 'Well, he'd have the patience for it, I'm sure.'

'But does he have the stomach?' Diane wrinkled her nose. 'Personally, I prefer mine nicely filleted from the fish shop.'

The two exchanged a grin and Geena felt her spirits lift. The weekend lay ahead. She wondered if she'd see anything of Jack.

Late on Saturday afternoon Geena was tamping down the last seedling into the new little flowerbed she'd created along her back fence, well aware she was killing time.

She'd had no word from Jack and guessed he was stuck in Sydney. Surely he could have rung? Stripping off her gardening gloves, she turned the hose on full blast to wash the stickiness off her hands and thought, Surely it doesn't take much effort to pick up a phone...

'Aha! Thought I'd find you here!'

'Jack!' Geena spun with a startled cry of pleasure, letting the hosepipe drop from her hand. It writhed like a snake, spraying water wildly.

Jack swore, jumping right and left, fending off the mini-storm with upraised arms. 'Where's the tap?' he yelled, making a futile attempt to stem the flow.

'Beside you. Near the fence.' Geena was doubled up with laughter, soaked and deliriously happy. He was back. Her hands grasping her knees, she watched as the water slowed to a dribble and then stopped. 'Are you OK?' she asked, holding a hand to her mouth.

The distance between them shrunk suddenly.

'I need a hug,' he growled, holding his arms out to her.

Geena hesitated. 'I'm all wet, jack.'

'I don't care.' He hauled her into his embrace.

They kissed long and thoroughly. 'God, I missed you!' Jack's eyes closed briefly and when they opened they were ablaze with need.

He threaded his fingers through her hair, holding her still. 'Put a few things together and come home with me, Geena.'

She swallowed. 'All right...' Lifting her hands, she touched the tiny creases beside his eyes. 'I'll have to change first.'

'OK, but be quick.' His eyes locked with hers, his meaning clear. 'I refuse to spend another night without you. Come on.' His hand stroked the rounded curve of her behind and he hurried her indoors. 'I'll help.'

Feeling light-headed, Geena grabbed clothes at random and disappeared into the bathroom to change.

He tapped on the door. 'No time for a shower, Geena. I want to get moving.'

She made a face at the closed door and did the best she could.

'Very fetching.' Jack laughed softly when she emerged, dressed in shorts and T-shirt, her hair still damp and standing up in little tufts.

'Very droll.' She showed him the tip of her tongue. In her bedroom she took up her brush and, with him watching amusedly, she reduced her hair to some kind of order. 'Better?' She flicked him a wry look.

'And better,' he emphasised, his eyes narrowing slightly. 'Geena?'

Her throat dried suddenly at the look on his face. 'Yes…?'

'Bring some clothes for work on Monday as well.'

Her heart hammering, she lifted a freshly ironed uniform on its hanger and placed it across the bed and then began throwing bits and pieces into a small overnight bag. Was that all she needed? Mentally she checked the contents and then turned and plucked her swimsuit from its hook behind the door.

'You won't need that.' Jack's voice was soft and he stayed her arm in midflight.

'Jack…' Her breath jammed in her throat. Swim nude? He must be joking!

'Come on, Geena.' His fingers captured her chin and turned it towards him. 'Live a little.'

'Jack…' She said his name again, this time with a hint of mild desperation.

'Think about it,' he said deeply. 'Tonight in the moonlight, the water like silk, our bodies without the barrier of clothes…'

Her breath caught and fire flooded her skin. 'Someone might come.'

He waved a dismissive hand. 'We'll hear them first. Besides, the dogs always bark at visitors.'

Feeling boneless, Geena plonked herself down on the end of the bed. 'We might have music on and not hear anything. And don't laugh!' she threatened, watching him slyly rub the back of his hand across his mouth.

'You're shy!' He laughed in disbelief, scooping her up from the end of the bed. 'And so sweet. That's why I love you. Now, come on.' He dropped a kiss on her surprised mouth. 'Let's grab what's left of the weekend.'

She went with him, her feet working automatically. 'That's why I love you.' He'd said the words jokingly, off the cuff. She wondered why suddenly she felt so vulnerable.

* * *

When they arrived at Wongaree they took her things straight up to his bedroom.

'I rang Helen earlier and asked her to air the place.' He put Geena's bag on the end table.

Her heart pounding, she slipped past him to hang her clothes in the wardrobe. 'It's a lovely room, Jack.' Slightly bemused, she looked about her. The colours were mostly greens and blues. She was surprised how well they seem to work with the white walls and old-fashioned glass lamps. 'Fresh and really...nice,' she added lamely, slightly shaken by the gentle power of its homeliness.

Jack lifted a shoulder. 'I organised a revamp of all the bedrooms before I moved in. You OK?' He was looking at her in a way that was unmistakable.

She licked her lips. 'I think so.'

'Then come here.'

She went to him. Willingly. Her heartbeat a tremolo of anticipation.

Sunday morning. Geena woke, early, lazily. She felt wondrously safe, protected, her arm hooked across Jack's back. She moved a little. 'Jack?'

'Morning.' He opened one eye. 'Sleep well?'

'Mmm.' She smiled, letting her fingertips drift up into the springy softness of his hair. 'I want to see your kookaburras.'

'Good grief!' he complained fuzzily, but even

with his back to her Geena could tell he was smiling.

She got her way.

They showered and dressed quickly and went downstairs to the kitchen.

'Do you feed them every day?' Geena leaned against the counter, watching, fascinated, as he got raw meat from the fridge and cut it into pieces.

He looked wry. 'Most days I don't get time but when I do I like to give them a treat. Come on.' His face settled into smiling lines. 'Let's see if they've arrived.'

She followed him outside and pretended to cover her ears. The shrillness of birdsong was almost deafening.

'Ah, there's our gang.' Jack placed several pieces of the meat on the timber railing and stood back.

Almost holding her breath in anticipation, Geena watched one cream and brown kookaburra edge along the railings and lean over curiously, before snatching the meat. 'What's he doing?' she asked, stifling a laugh as the bird gave his prize a whack against the railings before swallowing it.

'Much of their natural food is caught live.' He laughed softly. 'Like to feed one?'

Was he kidding? Geena took a quick step away. That beak looked as though it could wreak havoc on an unsuspecting finger. She looked him straight in the eye. 'Are you setting me up, Jack?'

'Would I?' He looked offended and then began to sing a snatch from 'Thank God I'm a Country Boy'.

'Very funny!' she retorted with a little sniff. 'All right.' She gritted her teeth and stared at the chunks of meat. 'Show me how.'

'Easy,' he joked, placing a piece of meat on the centre of her palm and holding it out.

With her eyes half-closed, Geena tensed and then opened her eyes wide in surprise when the meat was seized with hardly more than a nudge to her hand. 'That was brilliant!' She turned shining eyes on Jack. 'Let's do it again.'

'No.' He looked at her indulgently. 'Once we start, we'll never stop. These guys can be absolute tyrants.' Upending the dish, he tossed the rest of the meat out onto the grass and left them to it.

They breakfasted on warm muffins and coffee.

'You haven't told me about your meetings in Sydney.'

Jack's look was quick, speculative. 'They went well. Our request will go to committee first thing tomorrow. We may have an answer as early as Tuesday.'

Geena raised an eyebrow. 'You must have impressed them.' She toyed with the spoon in her saucer. 'And if we get the programme, what happens then?'

'The health department will let us have two fully

equipped mobile vans plus operatives. The idea may be to send one out to service the rural areas and leave one in town. We'll have to take our turn at staffing. Frequent short shifts appear the way to go.'

'Don't forget the parents will have to co-operate,' she warned.

He lifted a shoulder. 'They will. For most of them, neglecting to have their children inoculated has been an unfortunate oversight.'

'And not helped by lax attitudes from health professionals.'

'Agreed.' Jack's jaw tightened infinitesimally.

'Would you mind if I cooked us something special for dinner tonight?' Geena rose and began stacking their used crockery on a tray.

He waved a dismissive hand. 'Be my guest.'

'I thought I was,' she quipped, and dodged the serviette he tossed at her. 'I've had a peek in your fridge. You've got most of what I need for my menu. But I can improvise anyway.'

They shared a smile.

'Am I allowed to ask what we're having?'

'I'll surprise you.' Geena's teeth caught on her bottom lip. 'And you'll have to get out of my way now while I marinate.'

He held up his hands and backed away. 'Consider me gone. I'll be down at the stables if you need me.' He hugged her then let her go. 'I've the vet coming to look at one of the horses.'

She skipped across to the sink with the dishes. 'I thought you did your own horse-doctoring.'

'All the time.' He grinned and went out whistling.

Everything was ready. With a sense of satisfaction Geena surveyed her handiwork.

She'd set the smallish round table in the dining room. The tablecloth she'd unearthed was of the palest peach linen and she'd enhanced its simplicity with the rather ornate silver candlesticks.

Placing a jug of old-fashioned roses in the centre, she smiled. The whole exercise had been rather an adventure and she guessed Jack had no idea of the household treasures his mother had left behind—possibly for the next generation to enjoy.

Her lashes flickered down and then up. She wouldn't—couldn't—allow herself to indulge in that kind of conjecture. Nevertheless, she felt a little flutter of excitement as Jack appeared at the door and looked in.

He whistled softly and she grinned, ridiculously pleased. 'It all looks nice, doesn't it?' She lifted a hand and folded it across her chest. 'I explored the various cupboards...'

His look told her he didn't give a damn about

the cupboards. His eyes swept her from head to toe. 'You look stunning, Geena...'

Flushing slightly, she accepted his compliment. 'It's the kind of thing that rolls up and goes anywhere,' she said, fingering the slim-line skirt of her patio dress.

'That deep colour suits you perfectly.' Frowning, he moved into the room and switched on a lamp, creating a warm circle of light around them.

'Purple?' Geena gave a stilted laugh. 'It's supposed to denote power, isn't it?'

He looked at her moodily. 'On you, I would have thought *passion*.'

He went off to shower and change, leaving Geena knee-deep in confusion.

'Where did you learn to cook like this?' Jack asked as the dessert's tangy Jaffa flavour slid over his tongue.

Geena shrugged. 'Mum made sure we could all cook. I just took to it better than either Anne-Maree or Vanessa so I probably got to practise more.'

Slowly, he drew his gaze from his now-empty serving glass to her. 'If we chose, we could make this kind of thing a permanent arrangement.'

Geena parted her lips and then took refuge in flippancy. 'Heavens, I couldn't possibly rise to this standard all the time, Jack.' With fingers that shook, she crushed her serviette and dropped it beside her plate. 'After a day on the ward, you'd more than likely be looking at beans on toast!'

There was a short silence, then he said quietly, 'Marry me, Geena.'

Geena opened her mouth but nothing came out. She tried again. 'We're all right as we are, aren't we?'

His mouth hardened. 'I want us to be a proper unit, Geena. A married unit.'

Her stomach shook. 'That's a bit old-fashioned, isn't it?' Dear heaven, why was she talking herself out of it? Being married to him, it was what she'd dreamed about, longed for...

'I thought you loved me.' His jaw worked. 'Trusted me.'

'I do!' She blinked rapidly against the threatening tears clogging her throat. 'But marriage is—is such a huge responsibility.'

'And my track record is abysmal.' He stared broodingly at her across the jug of roses.

'Jack, don't...' Geena's hands curled into fists, her nails making small indents on the soft skin of her palms.

He snorted. 'Don't what? Hell, I've asked you to marry me, not jump off the Sydney Harbour Bridge!'

Maybe that would have been easier!

'I can't give you an answer now, Jack.' Sheer panic sharpened her words. What if, despite their best efforts, the marriage didn't work? After all, Jack's hadn't. Her parents' hadn't. And divorce rates were as high as the sky. But if she gave it her best shot—

'I can't talk about this now, Jack.' She jerked to her feet. 'I need some space.'

'I'll keep asking you, Geena,' he said tautly.

Her eyes clouded. 'I'll get the coffee.'

Dressed in her uniform Geena felt more in touch with herself. She looked up as Jack came into the kitchen, resolving there and then to treat it as a normal Monday morning.

Seeing him dressed casually but professionally in his cream cotton trousers, smoky grey shirt and red tie, drew everything into perspective.

'There's fruit and toast,' she said. 'And I've made tea. I wasn't sure if you wanted cereal.'

He shook his head. 'That's fine.' He turned and hefted Misty aside with his shoe. 'Have you fed the cat?'

A frown pleated her forehead. 'I wasn't sure what he ate.'

'Too much, if anything,' Jack growled, and proceeded to open a can of pet food. He called Misty out to the patio and left his food. Returning to the kitchen, he washed his hands and took his place at the table. 'You tossed and turned last night, Geena.'

Frowning, he selected a banana and began to peel it.

'Sorry.' Her mouth dried. If the truth be known, she hadn't wanted to share his bed at all. Instead, she'd have preferred to have been alone. Alone with her thoughts. Her sigh was long and broken. Perhaps she should just tell him now she'd marry him and have done with it, and let the future take them over.

'You look pale.' Jack's clinical gaze ran over her.

She almost choked. 'We probably didn't sleep very well.'

'No.' He looked moodily at her and then began to spread marmalade on his toast. 'I wonder why?'

Her eyes downcast, Geena felt a flush warm her skin. There'd been a terrible kind of desperation about their love-making which hadn't relaxed them at all. Afterwards, she'd lain awake, confused and just the tiniest bit afraid for them both.

A few minutes later Geena ran upstairs to clean her teeth, almost colliding with Jack as he emerged from the bathroom. He put his hand out to steady her. 'Is your bag ready?'

She nodded. 'On the end table.'

Snatching it up, he called over his shoulder, 'I'll get the car out. Slam the door after you, would you, please? It's self-locking.'

They were barely away from Wongaree when

Jack said, 'You seem a bit strung out, Geena. Have I jumped the gun?'

She stared at him blankly.

'By talking about marriage,' he clarified, frowning.

She caught her hands together in her lap. 'You did take me rather by surprise.'

'Why?' His dark brows lifted. 'I would've thought it was a natural progression.'

Geena shook her head. 'Don't you feel scared?'

He snorted. 'Of course I'm scared. I've been there once and made a hash of it, but that doesn't mean I'm not prepared to give it another shot. I have faith in us, Geena.'

She swallowed. 'I do too,' she whispered.

'Well, then?'

'Jack, please...' She gave an agonised little sigh. 'Just give me a bit of space.'

'I hate that expression,' he said, his blue blue eyes glinting. 'Either we're committed or we're not.'

Or maybe they were both grasping at straws. Her shoulders lifted in another sigh and she turned her head and looked out at the anthills that rose in pinky-brown symmetry along the fenceline.

That was how she noticed the bus.

'Jack! Stop!' She made a grab at his arm. 'Look over there. Isn't that the school bus?'

He jammed on the brakes, his gaze swivelling to

where she was pointing. What they saw horrified them both. One glance told them the yellow bus with its load of youngsters had careered off the road, taking the fence with it. From there it appeared to have rolled out of control into a deep culvert and was now only a hair's breadth from tipping completely on its side.

'Jack…' For a moment Geena thought she might be sick. 'Brenda's twins…'

'They may not have been picked up yet.' Nevertheless, he looked grim. He tossed her his mobile phone. 'Ambulance, police and fire brigade, Geena. Stat! I'll get my bag. And run!' he added, throwing open his door.

Geena made her call to the emergency number that co-ordinated the three services and was told they had already been alerted by a neighbouring farmer and were on their way.

'ETA?' she snapped.

'Five minutes.'

She snapped the aerial down and began running. The terrain was rough, all downhill, and she found it difficult to keep her footing. Jack was far ahead, his long legs having outstripped hers by a mile. Her breathing was beginning to hurt, and as she covered the last few metres wild scenarios juxtaposed in her head. Jack's safety meant everything.

'Jack…' She arrived panting beside him. 'Be careful. The whole thing might blow up…'

'It might, Geena.' His shoulders were straining as he tried to break the seal on the rear emergency window. 'It's a bit hard with only a pair of scissors and a screwdriver,' he said with dark humour, 'but I'm almost there. The cavalry coming?'

'Seconds away.' Shielding her eyes against the dazzling sun, she looked up and saw the children's faces peering down at them. They seemed to be smiling and some were waving. Geena's hand went to her throat. Please, heaven, they'd all be relatively unscathed. 'What about the driver?' she asked.

'Can't tell.' Jack's fingers peeled away more of the seal. 'Out of it, I'd say.'

The emergency services arrived with flashing lights and muted sirens, the appliance from the fire brigade stopping closest to the crippled bus.

Before it had completely stopped, a young fire officer had vaulted from the cabin. 'Morning, folks.' He offered a one-fingered salute, hitching himself up to see what progress Jack had made. He gave a wry grin. 'Nice try, Doc. But horses for courses, yeah?' He produced a special tool that ripped away the rest of the seal in seconds and the escape hatch was lifted out.

'OK, guys!' The young man stuck his head into the newly created cavity. 'Little kids first. Let's go!'

'We'll need to do a bit of triage here, Geena.' Jack said as a ladder was brought and the children were shepherded away to the shade of a tree. 'And let's hope someone's thought to bring water. It's got to be as hot as blazes inside that bus.'

Brenda's eight-year-olds, Liam and Joshua, were amongst the last out.

'Oh, Joshy!' Geena sprang forward. The little lad looked dazed, a bloodied hand covering his mouth.

'He's had a tooth knocked out.' A girl of high-school age, who seemed to have placed herself in charge of the twins, said quietly. 'It's hanging by a thread. I told him not to touch it and try to keep his mouth closed.' She looked anxiously from Jack to Geena. 'Was that OK?'

'That's excellent.' Geena was warm in her praise. She took the two boys into the shelter of her arms.

'I've just done my first-aid certificate,' the youngster said shyly.

'What about you?' Jack's keen eyes homed in on the girl's tightly held lips. 'Are you hurt at all?'

'Only my knees.' The student looked ruefully at her laddered tights. 'But it could've been heaps worse, couldn't it?' Her mouth trembled and tears began welling in her eyes. Impatiently she brushed them away.

With a reassuring hug Jack passed the youngster over to one of the female ambulance officers. He swore under his breath. Poor kids. They'd all need post-trauma counselling. It was to be hoped the schools involved came up with the goods as soon as possible.

'Is Mum coming?' Liam's little hand tugged at Geena's trousers.

Jack's gaze swung back to the trio. Geena. He swallowed the sudden lump in his throat. She'd make such a natural mother. Geena and kids. Geena and *his* kids. Not likely. His mouth firmed. She'd very conveniently stonewalled on that scenario.

'I think we'd do better to get you and Josh to your mum instead, young Liam,' Jack put his hand on the small boy's head. To Geena he said, 'Use the mobile and get on to Brenda, would you?' He glanced at his watch. 'She should be well and truly at the hospital by now.'

'This'll be difficult for Brenda,' Geena said quietly. 'Her husband's working in Saudi at the moment.'

'She'll cope.' Jack was blunt. 'Brenda doesn't have a negative bone in her body.'

Was that a not-too-subtle dig at her? Geena felt the heat on her skin. What had happened to their easy friendship, their lightness of spirit? The loving factor in their relationship? Right now, she couldn't see herself ever feeling truly comfortable with him again. It was all like picking her way through fog.

'I'll run a quick check on the boys.' Jack looked at her over their heads. 'And we should get Josh to a dental surgeon as soon as possible. I'll arrange to have both boys sent back in the first ambulance and perhaps Brenda could meet them at the surgery. Could you relay that to her, please?'

Geena took the mobile off her belt. They both knew that if Josh's tooth was to be saved, every second counted. But there was reason to be optimistic. By having kept the injured tooth in his mouth at body temperature, the nerves would have every chance of regenerating.

Geena looked about her and sighed. There seemed little more she could do for the moment. The details of the accident had travelled fast and many of the parents had already arrived at the scene to collect their offspring. And the children who were left were in the care of a WPC.

Freeing the driver, that had taken time, and precise metal-cutting equipment had been needed to get his door open. The emergency crew had rigged up a tarpaulin and Jack was now examining the injured man.

Walking slowly, Geena crossed back to the site, stopping at the periphery of the all-male group.

'How is he?' She directed her question to one of the ambulance officers, Jamie Sullivan.

'A couple of busted ribs apparently.'

Geena frowned. 'Do we know yet what happened?'

Jamie raised a hand and rubbed at his chin. 'Doesn't look too good. The doc's ordered a blood alcohol reading when we get him back to the hospital.'

'Do you mean he was drunk?' Her voice rose in shocked disbelief. 'They could have all been killed!'

'His wife's just left him, Geena.'

'That doesn't justify putting the lives of the children at risk!' Geena felt sick and angry. What was the world coming to?

CHAPTER ELEVEN

'WHAT will happen to him?' Geena's gaze followed the ambulance containing the injured driver as it left the scene.

'That's up to the police.' Jack's lower lip curled. 'He tried to tell me he'd blacked out. Passed out more like!'

She handed Jack his bag and slowly they retraced their steps up to the road and his Celica. When they reached the top of the incline she looked back. Except for the yellow bus, lying drunkenly in the ditch, she and Jack were the only ones left.

It was quiet. So quiet. Then a flock of plovers rose in a grey cloud from the wetlands, their querulous cries piercing the sudden peace.

'I'd kill for a shower.' Jack unlocked the car doors and they climbed in. The atmosphere inside was stifling. He sent her a quick look. 'Can you bear it for a while until the air-conditioning kicks in?'

'Sure.' Geena combed her fingers back through her hair. It had been the oddest start to the week and there was probably more drama to come. It would be all over the hospital by now that she'd spent the weekend with Jack at Wongaree.

Her sigh was long and shaky. Suddenly it seemed a bit pathetic to be even giving those kinds of thoughts head room. What had happened this morning and the bravery the children had shown had reduced everything to its right perspective.

Jack gave her a narrow look as he inserted the ignition key. 'Makes you believe there's a God out there somewhere when things like this happen, doesn't it?'

Geena swallowed. 'Someone was certainly looking out for those children.'

'What did we end up with?' He pressed the heels of his hands against his eyes and worked his shoulders for a minute. 'It all seems a bit of a blur now.'

A little sound tightened Geena's throat. 'Would you like me to drive, Jack? You must be exhausted.'

His blue gaze swung to her and widened. Her eyes were shadowed and faintly strained. He frowned. 'No more than you.' He started the car. 'Now, how did we end up?'

'Whiplash on several of the older kids.' Drawing in on herself, Geena's arms folded instinctively around her midriff. 'A sprained wrist. Various cuts and abrasions, one that needed stitching. And poor little Josh, of course.'

'What about ringing the hospital and see if there's been any word from Brenda?' he suggested.

* * *

'Let's call it a day, Julie.' Jack stripped off his lab coat and stuffed it in the bin.

'Won't be a tick.'

'Come on,' he cajoled, placing his hand in front of the computer screen. 'It's Friday afternoon. Pack it in.'

'OK, boss,' RN Julie Weston smiled and leaned back in her chair, her blonde, jaw-length bob almost touching his upper arm as she turned. 'We did a hundred and forty-five kids today, would you believe?'

Jack flexed his shoulders. 'I'd believe it all right.' He pushed her paperwork to one side. 'Are you bound for home this weekend?' The nurse was one of the health department team who had come from Sydney to help facilitate the inoculation programme.

'It's hardly worth the effort.' She put her hands to the back of her neck and massaged the muscles for a minute. 'By the look of things we'll be finished here by the middle of next week anyway. What about you?' She sent him a narrow green look. 'What are your plans for the weekend?'

'I think I'll wait and see what develops.' Jack retreated to the rear of the van.

Julie Weston gave him a speculative look as she got to her feet and swung her bag across her shoulder. The guy was a hunk but definitely a bit slow off the mark. She had a moment of inspiration.

'Some of us are meeting up for a drink at the pub about seven. Why don't you join us?'

Jack looked at her warily and she clicked her tongue. 'It's a birthday bash for one of the gang!'

'Ah...' He felt the tension drain out of him. What the hell was the matter with him lately? He was rapidly becoming antisocial. His mouth worked. He hadn't had a chance to talk properly to Geena in days but, then, she hadn't made any overtures either. He brushed a hand over his jaw. A few drinks with the visitors might be just the tonic he needed.

'Well, see you.' Julie waved brightly and swished out of the caravan.

'Julie!' Jack leapt to the door after her. 'What pub are you meeting at?'

The RN lowered her sunglasses and smiled up into his eyes. 'The Shearers' Rest. We'll be in the beer garden most likely.'

Jack pushed himself on through a late ward round. He was never going to make it to the pub. He glanced at the time. He still had to get home to shower and change.

An hour and a thousand second thoughts later he walked into the Shearers' Rest in uptown Hopeton. A wall of tropical fern, staghorns and elkhorns brushed against his arm as he made his way through the latticed-enclosed beer garden. The place was packed. But, then, it was Friday night, he reminded himself wryly.

He held his head high and cast his gaze around for his group. Eventually he spotted them, the mildly noisy crowd through the archway at the rear. He began making his way between the tables towards them, noticing they'd pulled several tables together and were arranged about them in one huge circle.

A smile on his lips, he recognised Julie's blonde head and most of the team from Sydney. And Piers and Tasha. Well, it was good to see them out and about. And Cassie animated as usual, with Brad hanging on her every word. And Geena. In her purple dress.

His heart nosedived. Why the hell hadn't he thought she might be here? He saw her flush and her nostrils pinch slightly as she saw him. His brows drew together in a frown. How on earth had things between them deteriorated to this kind of awkwardness?

He gave a general greeting around the circle and sank into the place Julie made for him next to her.

Geena swallowed the mouthful of food and felt it lodge heavily. Why on earth had she let Cassie bulldoze her into this evening? And just when she'd had ideas of slipping out unnoticed after the first round of drinks, they'd all begun ordering counter meals. Now she was stuck with a huge steak she didn't want and making a pretence of enjoying herself.

She prodded a chip on her plate. She'd never have expected Jack to have turned up here. Somehow she didn't think it was his scene at all. But, then, it was scarcely hers either.

She'd felt embarrassed to her soul, the centre of all eyes, when he'd sat down next to that blonde bombshell from Sydney...

'Herb bread?' Cassie shoved the basket in front of her. 'And cheer up, ducky. He's as miserable as sin over there.'

Geena tore at a piece of lettuce with her fork. 'What's that supposed to tell me?'

Cassie clicked her tongue. 'That he cares!'

'Huh!' Geena looked up spontaneously, catching his stare. She looked away, more confused than ever.

Eventually the plates were cleared but no one seemed to want coffee. Some people ordered more drinks, others opted for the dance floor.

A little bemused, Geena watched Brad whirl Cassie to her feet. Perhaps now she'd have an opportunity to cut and run.

Without warning, Jack put his hands on her shoulders. She stared up at him dazedly.

'Let's get out of here,' he said, abruptly.

'Where are we going?' she asked in a small voice as he urged her outside.

'Somewhere we can talk. This nonsense has gone far enough.'

The colour drained from her face. 'I'm not going home with you, Jack.'

He gave an exasperated snort. 'I said *talk*, Geena. Nothing else. Did you drive here?' His gaze shot over the parked vehicles.

'I came by cab.' She gave him a look of lofty disdain. 'I hardly finished my glass of wine anyway.'

He gave her a brief nod of satisfaction. 'I'm parked over here. Give me your hand.'

Geena found herself stealing a secret glance at him from time to time as they drove. She swallowed drily. 'Am I allowed to ask where we're going?'

'To the hospital.' He gave her a brief sideways glance. 'I want to check on a nine-year-old, Domica Palacios. She was admitted earlier this evening.'

'What's the problem?' Immediately Geena's caring instincts were aroused.

Jack frowned. 'As far as the parents could tell us, she fell off a practice trapeze wire.'

'Sorry?'

He lifted a shoulder. 'That was my initial reaction, too, but apparently the family is from the circus currently in town.'

'Oh, yes.' Geena bit her lip. 'I've seen the posters. How on earth did it happen?'

'Kids being kids, as far as I could gather. A few

of them were out of bounds, messing about while the adults were occupied elsewhere. Fortunately, it wasn't a high wire.'

Geena shivered. 'What's her prognosis? Is there cause for concern?'

'I'm being quite cautious,' he stated calmly, turning in at the hospital grounds. 'She has a goose egg on the back of her head and doesn't remember falling.'

'Thank heavens the parents had the sense to bring her in, then.' Geena was well aware that a period of observation for this kind of injury was of paramount importance. Any deterioration in the child's condition would be picked up immediately by professional monitoring.

'Will you X-ray?'

'Not yet.' Jack swept the Celica into his parking space. 'I'll leave my options open. Keep her for forty-eight hours.' He switched off the engine. 'Coming up?'

Geena rolled her eyes, sending a meaningful look between her purple dress and his black and silver shirt. 'As opposed to placing an announcement in the paper, do you mean?'

His mouth tipped and then he chuckled.

To Geena's ears it all sounded a bit rusty but at least it was there.

He switched the ignition back on. 'Play some music, then. I won't be long.'

* * *

'I haven't been here before.' Geena cast her eyes around the coffee lounge, taking in the soft colours of the decor, the patina of old wooden furniture, the glow from the copper lamps.

'Neutral ground,' Jack said succinctly. He bent his head over the menu. 'Any preference?'

Geena's heart was hammering. She doubted she'd be able to swallow anything. 'You choose,' she said.

'We'll order a pot of coffee, then,' he said decisively. 'And something to stoke up our energy. A serving of beesting cake. How does that sound?'

'Fattening,' she said, and gave him a shaky smile.

When the waitress had taken their order Jack leaned across the table and took her hand. 'It's been three weeks, Geena.' Turning her hand over, he stroked his fingertips across her palm.

Her breath caught as she looked at him.

'Dammit, Geena! What's changed?' His words were muted but nonetheless carried the force of his obvious frustration.

She swallowed hard. 'You took me unawares, Jack. I never thought you'd spring a marriage proposal on me. We hadn't been seeing one another that long.'

'That's rubbish! We've worked closely together for months now in a mostly taxing environment. If that's not a way of seeing the best and worse in each other, I don't know what is.'

She took a deep breath. He was right. Of course he was right and she knew she was playing for time. But time for what? she wondered bleakly. Time for things between them to become even more convoluted? She gently took her hand back. 'I'll try to explain it.'

The waitress arrived with their order at that moment and Jack said drily. 'We seem destined never to have this conversation. But let's eat first and talk later. OK?'

A little later Jack poured them each a second cup of coffee and waited. And waited. 'Talk to me, Geena.' His brows pleated blackly. 'I won't bite.'

She looked down at her hands clasped in her lap, her sense of purpose wavering. 'You'll probably think I'm paranoid.'

'No, I won't,' he said softly. 'Trust me.'

She took a deep breath. 'What if our marriage didn't work out?'

'We'd work at it,' he responded evenly. 'Make sure it did.'

She made a little throw-away motion with her hand. 'There's nothing to say one of us wouldn't run off if it got too hard, though, is there?'

Jack rubbed his forehead thoughtfully. 'Am I right in assuming all this goes back to your own family situation? Your father leaving?'

'He wasn't noted for his staying power,' she stated bitterly.

'Which means you'd try twice as hard to make your own marriage work, doesn't it?'

'Of course I'd try,' she said tightly. 'But there are no guarantees, Jack. You told me that yourself.'

For a long moment he just looked at her, his gaze never wavering. 'Just where is all this leading, Geena? Are you giving me the boot?'

'No!' She looked shocked. 'That's not what I'm saying at all!' Her lips trembled slightly. 'I'm just scared, Jack. Scared to death.'

He took her hand and held it tightly. 'Aren't you forgetting one thing, Geena? I'd be there with you. We'd be a team. It takes two to make and keep a marriage going—'

'And only one to make it fail,' she cut in. She saw his eyes narrow and went on quickly. 'I was there when my father left, Jack. My mother cried but he went anyway.'

'Did you ever ask her why they split up?'

She blinked. 'I tried once. When I was about sixteen. I didn't get anywhere. Mum got terribly upset. Said she'd done the very best she could. And hadn't I been happy? We *were* a happy family,' she insisted, her eyes suddenly glazing with tears.

Silently, Jack handed her his handkerchief. 'Do you have some leave due?' he asked abruptly.

'I suppose…' she said huskily. 'A week—maybe two.'

'Then go and see your mother, Geena. Get some answers.'

Her eyes widened. 'But I—'

'Get some answers,' he repeated. 'Or I will.'

CHAPTER TWELVE

It took several days for Geena to organise her leave and then she was gone.

When she returned a rush of nerves assailed her as she walked on the ward for her usual early shift. Her team welcomed her back with open arms. And flowers.

'We're Bouquets and Blossoms's best customers now,' Krista said cheekily, handing over the huge bunch of vividly coloured gerberas. 'And no one deserves these more than you, Geena.'

'Hear, hear,' someone echoed.

Overcome, Geena looked around the smiling faces. 'They're gorgeous. Thank you, everyone. I feel as though I've been away for a year instead of a couple of weeks,' she said with a laugh.

Piers caught her eye and winked. 'Tasha's back at work.'

'Oh, that's brilliant!'

'And taken Daniel in hand,' Megan put in with a sincerity that spoke of heartfelt relief. 'He can't believe what's hit him.' She grinned. 'Tasha's just about got him mobile. And wonder of wonders.' She paused for effect. 'He's forgotten how to complain!'

There was laughter all round.

'Oh, Brenda.' Geena's head was whirling with happiness. 'How's Josh doing?'

'Really well,' the older woman said cheerfully. 'He's to see a dental specialist in Sydney during the next school holidays. But so far so good.' Her eyes softened. 'You look better for your break, Geena.'

'I am,' Geena said. 'I feel terrific.' Then she looked up and saw Jack.

It was another half-hour before she could get to him. Her heart thumping, she tapped on his door and went in. 'Jack...'

Bent over his work, it seemed an eternity before he raised his head. 'Hello, Geena.'

'I've a lot to tell you,' she said with a little smile.

He nodded. 'Everything OK?'

'Yes... Could we go home together after work?'

He leaned back, folding his arms. 'Home as in Wongaree?'

She nodded and his eyes glinted with satisfaction.

'I'll push through here early,' he said. 'Pick you up about five.'

'So, my love, can you tell me now?' Jack smudged a kiss across her temple. They were in his bed, the curtains drawn against the last rays of a brilliantly setting sun.

She laughed softly. 'That was some homecoming, Doctor.'

'Creative,' he murmured. His eyes caressed her tenderly. 'And that was just the beginning. Comfortable?'

'Mmm.'

'Go on, then. Did you talk to your mum?'

'Yes. And my dad…' she said, hardly able to contain her smile.

His head turned and they lay there, looking at each other. 'So…' He let his breath go softly, his eyes opening wide. 'Tell me more.'

Geena moved a fraction and kissed his shoulder. 'I tackled Mum as soon as I got home. She didn't seem surprised. She said she'd more or less been waiting for me to ask her again. She said it was as much her fault as Dad's that they split up. That she'd never really wanted what he did.'

'And what did he want?' Jack asked, picking up her hand and kissing the tips of her fingers.

'To travel. Experience life in other places. But, of course, they had no money for that kind of indulgence. Then one day something happened and Dad had the chance of a job in Hawaii. It was for an American company and would have included his family.'

'But your mother wouldn't go.' Jack's voice became serious.

'No. She said the thought of it was like a nightmare for her. She wanted the safety of her small world, her three little girls... Dad couldn't talk her round.'

'So he went?'

'Yes. But he came back a year later. He went to Mum's work to try to persuade her to go back with him. But she said it was all too late...'

'Did he not try to see his girls?'

Geena sighed. 'Mum assured him we were settled. He didn't want us torn between their different worlds.'

'How sad.'

'Yes,' she agreed huskily. 'He also sent money I never knew about.'

There was a long silence broken only by their breathing and then she resumed speaking. 'Mum had his phone number in Honolulu. I rang him, Jack. I—didn't know what to expect, how it would be. But I had to try!'

'Of course you did.' Her small sob tore right through him. He gathered her into his arms, cradling her gently, his cheek against hers. 'You're my brave lady.'

She sniffed. 'He was so pleased to hear from me. Over the moon really. And he's married again. His wife's called Moana. And I have a half-brother, Luis. He's seventeen...'

She cried then, tears of relief and happiness all rolled into one.

After a long time Jack said quietly, 'Are you OK?'

She hiccuped through a throaty laugh. 'It just seems to have hit me now. I have a real family.'

'Would you like them to come to our wedding?' Jack's lips found hers, gentle and undemanding.

'Probably not.' She hesitated. 'It might all be a bit awkward. And Mum would be hurt. But if you wouldn't mind...' she said, winding her fingers into his hair.

'Anything, Geena. You know that.'

'Well...I wonder if we could have a trip to Honolulu for our honeymoon?'

Jack propped himself up on one elbow and looked at her. 'It would be my pleasure to take my wife.'

'Can we afford it?'

'Of course we can.' He kissed her playfully, once, twice, three times. 'I'll do my doctoring twice as hard. Make twice as much money.'

'Jack. I'm serious!'

'Me, too.' He grinned. 'Seriously in love with you. When can we get married?'

'Oh, heavens! I don't know. A month? Six weeks?'

He chuckled. 'Belinda will want to bring you back a wedding dress from Rome.'

Geena raised her eyebrows. 'Now that would be just a tad expensive.'

'Not for Belle. She'll know a little man who will do her a good deal.'

'I'm so looking forward to meeting her.' Geena's voice trembled slightly. 'And all your family.'

'Me, too. Meeting yours.' He brushed a kiss across her mouth. 'The whole box and dice.'

'And we'll have huge family gatherings from time to time.' Her heart was overflowing. 'And we'll always make Valentine's Day our special day.'

'We will?' He looked startled. 'What should I try to remember?'

'Idiot,' she said softly. 'Our first kiss, of course. I love you, Jack.' Her solemn look spoke volumes. 'We will be all right, won't we?'

'You bet we will. Believe it, Geena,' he murmured, trailing his hand down her back, pulling her even closer against him. 'Believe in the heart.'

MILLS & BOON®

Makes any time special

Enjoy a romantic novel from
Mills & Boon®

Presents...™ *Enchanted*™ TEMPTATION®

Historical Romance™ MEDICAL ROMANCE®

MILLS & BOON

MEDICAL ROMANCE

THE GIRL NEXT DOOR by Caroline Anderson
Audley Memorial Hospital

When surgeon Nick Sarazin and his two children, Ben and Amy, moved next door to ward sister Veronica Matthews, she helped as much as possible. It was clear to Ronnie that Nick had yet to let go of his wife's memory, and there'd only be heartache, loving this beautiful man...

THE MARRIAGE OF DR MARR by Lilian Darcy
Southshore # 3 of 4

Dr Julius Marr had been deeply impressed by Stephanie Reid's care of her mother, but afterwards he didn't know how to stay in touch—until he could offer her the job of receptionist at the practice. But until he'd tied up some loose ends, they couldn't move forward.

DR BRIGHT'S EXPECTATIONS by Abigail Gordon

Nurse Antonia Bliss first met paediatrician Jonathan Bright when she was dressed as the Easter Bunny! Was that why he thought she couldn't know her own mind? But his own expectations were so battered, he needed some excuse to keep her at a distance...

0002/03a

Available from 3rd March 2000

Available at most branches of WH Smith, Tesco, Martins, Borders, Easons, Volume One/James Thin and most good paperback bookshops

MILLS & BOON

MEDICAL ROMANCE

A SON FOR JOHN by Gill Sanderson
Bachelor Doctors

Since qualifying Dr John Cord had concentrated on work, trying to forget that he had loved and lost his Eleanor. But his new Obs and Gynae job brought her back into his life. Even more shocking was the sight of a photo on Ellie's desk of a young boy who was clearly his son!

IDYLLIC INTERLUDE by Helen Shelton

Surgeon Nathan Thomas borrowed his step-brother's Cornish cottage, only to find himself next door to a beautiful girl. Not one to poach, Nathan was horrified by his instant attraction to nurse Libby Deane, assuming she was Alistair's girlfriend.

AN ENTICING PROPOSAL by Meredith Webber

When nurse Paige Warren rescued a young Italian woman, she phoned Italy leaving a message for 'Marco', but Dr Marco Alberici—an Italian prince!—arrives in person, disrupting her surgery and her hormones! Should she really accept his invitation to return to Italy?

Available from 3rd March 2000

Available at most branches of WH Smith, Tesco, Martins, Borders, Easons, Volume One/James Thin and most good paperback bookshops

FREE!

4 Books
and a surprise gift!

We would like to take this opportunity to thank you for reading this Mills & Boon® book by offering you the chance to take FOUR more specially selected titles from the Medical Romance™ series absolutely FREE! We're also making this offer to introduce you to the benefits of the Reader Service™ —

- ★ FREE home delivery
- ★ FREE gifts and competitions
- ★ FREE monthly Newsletter
- ★ Books available before they're in the shops
- ★ Exclusive Reader Service discounts

Accepting these FREE books and gift places you under no obligation to buy; you may cancel at any time, even after receiving your free shipment. Simply complete your details below and return the entire page to the address below. **You don't even need a stamp!**

YES! Please send me 4 free Medical Romance books and a surprise gift. I understand that unless you hear from me, I will receive 6 superb new titles every month for just £2.40 each, postage and packing free. I am under no obligation to purchase any books and may cancel my subscription at any time. The free books and gift will be mine to keep in any case.

MOEB

Ms/Mrs/Miss/Mr ....Initials....................
BLOCK CAPITALS PLEASE

Surname..

Address...

....

....Postcode ....

Send this whole page to:
UK: The Reader Service, FREEPOST CN81, Croydon, CR9 3WZ
EIRE: The Reader Service, PO Box 4546, Kilcock, County Kildare (stamp required)

Offer not valid to current Reader Service subscribers to this series. We reserve the right to refuse an application and applicants must be aged 18 years or over. Only one application per household. Terms and prices subject to change without notice. Offer expires 31st August 2000. As a result of this application, you may receive further offers from Harlequin Mills & Boon Limited and other carefully selected companies. If you would prefer not to share in this opportunity please write to The Data Manager at the address above.

Mills & Boon is a registered trademark owned by Harlequin Mills & Boon Limited.
Medical Romance is being used as a trademark.

MILLS & BOON®

Makes Mother's Day special

For Mother's Day this year, why not spoil yourself with a gift from Mills & Boon®.

Enjoy three romance novels by three of your favourite authors and a FREE silver effect picture frame for only £6.99.

Pack includes:

Presents...
One Night With His Wife by Lynne Graham

Enchanted
The Faithful Bride by Rebecca Winters

TEMPTATION®
Everything About Him by Rita Clay Estrada

Available from 18th February